MW01712073

When In Elora

By: Kaitlin Colicchio

When In Elora 0
Chapter 1: The Beginning 2
♦ ♦ ♦ 29
♦ ♦ ♦ 38
Chapter 3: The Aftermath 38
♦ ♦ ♦ 50
Chapter 4: The First Day **50**
♦ ♦ ♦ 57
Chapter 5: The Friendship 57
♦ ♦ ♦ 69
Chapter 6 The Carnival 69
♦ ♦ ♦ 88
Chapter 7: The Family Boat 88
♦ ♦ ♦ 119
Chapter 8: The Tea Party 119
♦ ♦ ♦ 125
Chapter 9 The Summer 125
♦ ♦ ♦ 132
Chapter 10: The Family Reunion 132
♦ ♦ ♦ 146
Chapter 11 The Bonfire 146
♦ ♦ ♦ 162
Chapter 12: The Last Day 162
♦ ♦ ♦ 169
Chapter 13: The Reunion 169

♦ ♦ ♦ 180
Chapter 14: The Wedding *180*
♦ ♦ ♦ 190
Epilogue *190*
Bonus Chapter *196*
♦ ♦ ♦ 202

To my friends who never told me to go away with all my ideas,

Thank you for every idea you listened to and the continuous changes I made along the way. Without the help from every one of you - this wouldn't have been possible.

"We lay in each other's arms for hours, looking up into the sky. We laughed and pointed out shapes we could make out in the stars. Until we realized it was almost midnight, and the bugs started swarming. That was my favourite night we spent together. I knew he had stolen my whole heart.

WHEN IN ELORA

Chapter 1: The Beginning

15 June 2021

Present

It's so freakin' cold, and I don't want to be here. The time is 3 am, and I'm more than drunk, if that's possible. Why am I here if I don't do this? I stumble through Toronto's streets, and it's part of the drunk girl experience. The cold breeze rushes into my lungs with every breath I take. Exhaling, I see my breath and hear my teeth chatter. There's nowhere to go; I've got a bottle in my hand, my legs are getting tired, and my attention is drawn to the subway sign with the stairs leading down. So I follow them. There's nobody around but a homeless man sleeping on a bench about 10 feet away. I can hear the sound of cars a few streets away and the occasional snore from the bench-man, but besides that, it's quiet. I sit on the nearest bench to me and make myself comfortable because why not? My ass is freezing, but I don't care. Deep down in my heart- this feeling is much worse than the numbing tingles of a cold ass.

Today was going to be a good day. It should have been a great day. But I'm a coward, and I backed out. I didn't show up. Instead of running into the arms of the man I love, I watched too much Netflix, overate ice cream and drank my sorrows away. I am drunk and alone in a stinky subway at three in the morning.

I hear voices in the distance, drunk people laughing in the streets and footsteps hitting the concrete, the bench man still snoring. How did I get here? Wait. I know how I did. Jay and Mila said I needed to, and I quote, 'grow up and put my big girl panties on.' The thing is, though, decisions like this are complex. It's been three years since I last saw him; things could be different now. I can't get my heart shattered all over again and, of course, my superstitions that have followed me around since, forever.

I sit for what feels like hours in my thoughts. Battling myself to get on the train right then and there. 'I'll get the next one or the next one.'

I think of him until my vision goes blurry, and I feel myself slip into a deep sleep as I slide down into the bench and put my arm under my head like a pillow. I close my eyes. "*I love you. There I said it. I love you, Olive.*" "*What? Carter, you sure?*" "*Yes, baby, I love you. You are it for me. I don't care if it's only been a few months*; it's *been the best summer of my life. I've never felt like this before.*" "*I love you, but….*"

"S'cuse me, miss! Miss! Are you okay?"

My eyes dart open, and I take a massive gasp of cold air with my screech; it fills my lungs. I look up, and standing above me is an old lady, short and cute. She has shoulder-length hair that seems dark at some point, but it's grown over with gray. She's all bundled up, clinging to her purse. "Well,….. Miss, are ya gonna let me take a seat or make this poor old thang stand and wait for the train?" It takes me a minute to realize how I had even got there in the first place. I grab my phone from my pocket, and it reads 6:48 am; I shove it back in my pocket and shake my head in disbelief.

"Sor..sorry. Of course." I sit up and slide over, my head touching my knees. My head is throbbing, and my throat is dry.

"You okay, little lady?" She opens her purse, pulls out aspirin, and hands me a water bottle. "Here. Take this." She says. She eyes me like *Don't worry*; I'm *not a killer.* I take it like she's my mother telling me what to do. She'd always pop out of nowhere when I felt ill as a child and into my teen years. 'Here, take this. Do this, do that. Don't forget to drink your water.' Nagging. But at this point, I feel too shitty to care about that or that this sweet old lady could be some undercover spy or a killer.

"Fuck. Thanks. I feel like shit." I replied. She laughs.

“I'm 72; I come prepared for all aches and pains these days” She raises an eyebrow, glances toward me, and then smiles.

“You know, I don’t normally do this.” I wave my hand around the empty bottles surrounding me on this filthy subway bench. “It seems that no matter where life takes me, it always comes back to him. I have a decision to make — and that decision can change the whole trajectory of my life. It’s just, I don't know, what if it’s not the *right decision*?” I start to weep. “Sorry, I'm rambling to a stranger now,” I add.

“Oh, sweetheart. That's the thing; you never know if it’s the *right* decision. All I can say is, follow your heart because it always leads you to where you need to go.” I sigh. She's right, but I don’t want to hear it. I hear the train's roar in the distance, and fully knowing this embarrassing moment would end, it was a sigh of relief. She stands up. “Agnus, my name's Agnus, by the way.” She smiles and holds out her hand.

“Nice to meet you. I’m Olive.” I stand up and smile and place my hand into hers with a gentle shake. She opens her mouth as if she wants to say something but doesn’t. She turns and walks away, and I sit back down and grunt in dismay. Before she steps onto the train, I notice her stop in her tracks from the corner of my eye.

"You know, Olive, I don't have anywhere I need to be. I was heading out to shop for ingredients to bake my grandchildren some pies. But that can wait." She adds. I laugh,

"To get ingredients to bake a pie at this hour? That's some real love right there, Agnus." I smile.

"I do what I can these days. Anyways, maybe if you talk about it, it'll make you feel better. What do you think? Tell me your story, and I sure as heck can try to give you my two cents. Plus, it'll give me something to do." I'd think she was shipped from above if I didn't know better. I mean, who wants to waste time listening to my story? But I don't care because, honestly, I'm desperate.

"I appreciate the kindness, but I don't think you'd want to hear my story… It's sort of messy."

"Now, I may be old, but I'm no prude. It's not like I live a wild life these days, but I haven't always lived a tame life either." Agnus giggles the sweetest giggle and winks. I sit, slide over, and look toward the empty spot next to me, motioning her to sit down. "How about Let's get you some coffee, shall we?" she looks behind me, shocked. Like she had just seen a ghost.

I jump to my feet to look behind, seeing the bench man from earlier peeing all over the wall next to us. He starts yelling, "GO AWAY! THIS IS MY

BENCH." Jesus Christ. I pull the change out of my pocket and put it on the bench,

"Sorry, dude.." I say as I back away slowly. I gestured for Agnus to walk ahead of me and then look back; I looked at Agnus and said, "Let's get out of here."

"Weirdo," The man peeing in the corner says to me and then; huffs, he pulls up his pants and zips up the zipper and shoots us a devilish grin as he tries to make his way closer to us, but it's clear he is intoxicated and cannot walk. I can't help but shake my head and keep walking. Seeing this is normal in the streets of Toronto, so I'm used to this. it's best not to engage and keep moving.

"Let's go!" I motion Agnus toward the stairs leading outside the train station. We hurry up the steps and finally go outside.

"Oh, dearie, that was quite something, wasn't it?" She lets out a booming laugh, then coughs and stands in place.

"Okay, let's get you inside somewhere warm. Have you ever been to Kay's?" I ask.

Looking up, we stand out in front of Kay's Diner. It's probably one of the most underrated diners in town. We live in Toronto, Ontario. It's so fast here that If you stop, you might just get run over. We hurry inside the doors, and Doreen looks up from behind the counter.

"Take a seat, Ollie! Be there in a minute," she yells and points toward the booth open in her section. Doreen likes to call me by a nickname. The walls are bright yellow, covered in black and white photos of everyone from Marilyn Monroe and Elvis Presley to any famous band or icon you can think of. Incandescent light bulbs were hanging over each table, old-fashioned boom boxes to the sides, and the outfits servers wore, it felt like you stepped into the 60s. They wore yellow dresses with white aprons and gave Audrey Hepburn vibes.

They have the best-scrambled eggs. I don't know if they sprinkle magic dust on them back there, but they are *amazing*. I guide Agnus to her seat and then sit opposite her. Once we are settled, Doreen comes behind the counter with a menu and a coffee. She knows my order because I'm a regular here. I'm not much of a cook, I wouldn't say I *hate* grocery shopping, but it's not high up on the list of things I like to do.

I act like I won't get the same thing every time I'm here: scrambled eggs, three pieces of bacon, and two pieces of toast. If I feel extra adventurous, I get some fruit on the side. Breakfast is always the same. It's safe. I wait a few minutes before shutting the menu and placing it on the table. "I'm just going to have coffee for now," I say to Agnus,

"I'll take some water," Agnus replies. "I'll be right back, dear." She heads for the bathroom. Doreen comes over, and I order water for Agnus.

"You doing okay, Ollie?" Doreen looks concerned.

"Ahh, I'm alright. Don't worry about me." I replied. She looked at me for a few seconds before I forced a half-ass smile
and said, "Seriously, I'm okay."

"If you need. Anything…"

"Call you, got it! Thanks, Doreen." I grab my coffee and take a sip as the burn goes down my throat. "Ahhhh." When I look up, Doreen is gone, and Agnus slips back into her seat.

"So why are you out this early?" I ask Agnus with concern. "It can't just be the pies."

'I get bored sitting all alone in my house. My husband passed away two years ago, and things haven't been the same since…." Agnus' demeanour shifts, and she now seems sad and broken.

"I'm sorry… I shouldn't. I'm sorry." Sadness fills the space, so I try to shift the energy, "Well, you came all the way here with me, I guess I should explain."

"Only when you're ready." She smirks.

Pull my jacket off, shift my bum into the booth chair and get comfortable. "Not sure where to start…."

"From the beginning." She says

Past

It all began on my life's best and worst days. But before we start that, I'll explain how I got there. I eagerly awaited a call back for a job to help manage an aquarium. At the same time, all my friends back home in Toronto had grand plans for their summer before college started back up. I'm 22, so many of my friends are already mid-way through their college programs or finished, whereas I have been floating around since I graduated High School almost four years ago. For eight months, I believed I'd be an English major, and I started taking night school and summer courses to improve my skill. I found it so dull I couldn't keep up. Marine Biology was my passion; it's what drives me to want to go to work or school.

My biological father, Kenneth, passed away when I was twelve. I didn't know him; we weren't close during childhood. He was so consumed with his life and career that I was last in his mind. He sent Christmas and Birthday cards, but that was about it. My grandma Rosa reached out when he passed - she wanted to meet me in person. So we made it an annual trip; Mom and I would fly out there once a year for a week - after the first few years, Mom stopped coming, and I would meet Grandma Rosa at the airport.

I learned a lot about my dad during those summer trips. Who he was, what drove him to be who he was. All he wanted to do was save wildlife, and he dedicated his 54 years of life to it until he succumbed to stomach cancer, and ultimately his life was cut short. It was the summer of 2017, and Mom and Richard wanted to take a trip to see his side of the family, and Grandma Rosa suggested I visit her for the entire summer instead of a week. After sitting on it for a few days and speaking to Mila and Jay - they told me to do it, "Live a little." They said,

During the summer of 2017, I visited my paternal family. Not just a week this time, but the entire summer. During my summer there, I learned a lot about Kenneth; I got to work alongside exceptional people at Vancouver Aquarium. There, I worked with African Penguins and Sea otters. I overheard workers' conversations about these animals' dangers and became obsessed with helping them. I spent days upon days at this place;

I didn't want to leave their side. Grandma Rosa told me I reminded her of Kenneth and that he would've been so proud that we shared similar interests.

It took me a while to figure out that I needed to follow my passion for myself and take this material gain of doing what I thought I had to do and just do what I wanted to instead.

My friends always managed to make grand plans during the summer holidays.

On the other hand, I had plans to get out of town and do anything that did not involve being on a dull, sunny beach, drinking the days away.

There's this small town called Elora, two hours outside of Toronto. The town of 10299 people has an Elora Reef aquarium, which has become run down over the years. There were things there that interested me. The most important being that it wasn't in Toronto. It's far enough away from my family and my ex. Sometimes I felt suffocated at home, and I just needed a break - but until then, I didn't allow myself to do so. My best friend and I called my ex 'Asshole,' but his friends call him Tanner. Anyway, I wanted to escape all of that nonsense.

I wanted to help this place, and my experience at the Aquarium in Vancouver gave me an advantage. At a minimum, it would look good on my resume.

They desperately needed to get this place back to standards to keep it from closing. Kenneth abandoned my mom when she was pregnant with me, and my mother isn't a fan that I have the same interests as him. I couldn’t fight this urge to get up and leave, though, escape for a little while.

Elora Reef responded to my application almost instantly, which relieved me; I also worried I might be in over my head. I was due to leave at the beginning of June and spend my summer in the township of Elora, working at the Elora Reef; I felt good and happy. I had something to look forward to.

Elora Reef opened its doors in 1934 when Brimley Coral and his family had pets of all kinds, and he had a knack for healing animals. Call it what you want, but he was a vet. His friends and family called him Dr. Healer. When his home became overcrowded, he built something he could call his own. That's when Elora Reef came in. It was unusual in that period for people to own that many pets, but he made money from it instead of being ashamed of it. Brimley and his family used to charge 25 cents to come up and pet his snakes, turtles and other weird amphibians. When they finally made enough money, he and his family opened the aquarium. So he no longer had to work from home, and he could expand and, in doing so - help more animals. It went down through generations and, over time, wound up in Ronnie's lap, Randy Ronnie Coral.

Their story is a tale of time, so my heart was set on that place. I packed my bags, and I didn't look back. Even when my friends from school would message each other in our group chats, begging me to stay and talking about all the parties they would go to while I was gone. All the people could wait, and as much as I could enjoy a margarita or two, this was important to me, and I needed change and distance to gather my thoughts. After all, I did, and even though it had only been a few months, I was trying to move forward.

'Out with the old, in with the new,' they say.

I was so excited the day I left I didn't even wait - I woke up and grabbed my coffee to go; Mom had been sitting at the kitchen table reading her paper when I snuck past and said, "I'll see you, mom!" I bent over and kissed her head,

"What's the rush? Have some breakfast, Olive." She insisted.

"Can't? I want to get out - beat the morning traffic." Before she had time to answer, I snuck out the door lugging my bags when Richard ran behind me, grabbing my things,

"Olive, always ask me first, sweetie!" Rich has always been my dad. He raised me my entire life, and I love him more than words describe him. He's always gone above and beyond to help me, to be the dad I deserved.

"Thanks, Dad. I love you." I rush into my car door, slamming it behind me.

"Ol!" My dad shouts, shrugging his shoulders. "I told you, you're going to break that door. You can shut it without slamming it." He rolled his eyes but blew a kiss my way.

"Yeah, yeah. Okay, bye, Dad." I turn the radio on the 80's pop station and pull out of the driveway.

I got this.

Before my arrival, I had researched this place extensively, but nothing could've prepared me for what I walked into. I arrived there a day early to get settled. There was a small Inn down the road from the Aquarium, so I planned to stay at the Elora Inn for the entire summer. It was friendly, with a musty smell, but nothing a Charmed Aroma candle couldn't fix.

I wanted to check out the Aquarium the day of my arrival, even though it was only Saturday and I wasn't expected to start until Monday. I wanted to give myself at least a day to explore before I started working at Elora Reef. I threw my long brown waves into space buns, put some gloss on, and threw on my favourite high-waisted pants and a cute pink crop top with a Twenty-One Pilots logo. I found my white converse, slipped them on, and headed for the door.

I put the address into my phone to find the fastest walking route in minutes. I took my time getting there, taking in my surroundings. It was nice being there, and people seemed happy. It was quiet; you'd hear the faint sound of children playing, water splashing, and laughter filling the silence. I approached the building of the aquarium, and it was certainly run down over the years, more than it was in the photos I had found on google - so they must've needed to be updated. I've never backed down from a challenge though anything was better than being back home at that moment. I was committed.

I approached the building. The outside was beautiful; aside from all the wear and tear over the years, I could see its magic and picture how it looked before all the decay. It had a dark brick with tall pillars on either side that formed an arch, and in gold letters, it read "Coral Reef." The building was wrapped in bright green vines of Ivy, and the front doors were made of glass. I pulled open the door and walked in. The inside doesn't quite compare to the exterior details. But I didn't focus on that. I'm not here to decorate. To the left of me was a desk with a girl around my age sitting on a chair behind it. She didn't notice me walking in since her face was glued to her phone. I pretended to cough to get her attention, so I didn't have to approach her first.

"Oh, hi!" She jumped up and squealed. "How can I help you?"

"Hi, yeah..... Sorry, I'm Olive. I got in today and wanted to check out the place." I replied, "Nice to meet you."

"Oh, Olive! You're the new girl, right?" She came out from behind the desk and approached me.

"Yes, sorry again. I didn't mean to intrude." I replied,

"No problem at all, girl; if you need anything, let me know! Should I show you around? Let me find Ronnie for you." She walked off, and I stood there waiting. On the desk, I noticed a flyer sitting on top. In big, bolded yellow letters on a black background, it read, "**Elora Spring Fair"** Call me intrigued, but I started to read all the little details in smaller notes to the bottom.

"It seems he's left early, but he'll be here tomorrow if you want to come by and meet him before your first shift" Nancy approached beside me, looking at me, looking at the flyer.

"You should come." She glanced up at me since she stood one or two inches shorter than me. "To the fair."

"Oh, yeah. Maybe I will." I replied awkwardly.

"Everyone goes. All the proceeds go back into the town. You should come! It's at the harbourfront." She was talking so fast she barely took a breath.

"Yeah, that sounds nice. I think I will. I wanted to get to know the town since I'll be here all summer." I replied. Nervous but also excited.

"Yay! Here. Put your number in my phone. My girls and I will meet you there." Hesitantly I put my number into her phone and handed it back to her. She started walking further into the aquarium and gestured for me to follow.

"Ronnie will go through everything with you when you come in on Monday. He's a sweetheart. Loves these animals more than anything, and he's holding on to this place like his life depends on it." I nodded as I scanned the place as we walked through.

"Anyway, gotta go, girl. Time to do my rounds. Cya later, yeah?"

"Sounds good."

"And, Olive? I know this place seems run down, and it is. But Ronnie is a good person, and we want this place to work out for him. So, thanks." I smiled as I watched Nancy bobble her way out the front door. It was hard to imagine this girl working here. I'm not one to judge, but she gave me the whole '*I'm better than you'* vibe with her long bright blonde hair and lipstick as red as the loudest crimson. Suffice it to say; she didn't fit in a place like this. I shrugged off the bad vibe; I didn't want to ruin a potential friendship that could be good before I'd even given her a shot. I made my way through the building to explore everything I could.

Minutes turned into hours; I hadn't realized the time until my phone rang, and it was Mom; I clicked ignore because I could just call her later, and I did that often - but only because my Mom talking on the phone turns into hours, not just minutes. I noticed how hungry I was, so I made my way back to the Inn, and in a swift 8 minutes. I began pulling out food I had shoved into my mini fridge and made a sandwich. I plopped onto the bed and turned the TV on, and clicked on the first thing I saw, Gilmore Girls. Perfect. I picked up my phone and had text messages filling my screen. I clicked the top one. First,

Mila

So, how is it?

Text me when you can. I want to know how you are!

helllllllo????

Me

Hey. Sorry. I'm good. I was touring the aquarium. This town's somewhat cool but creepy. I miss you guys already. Promise you'll come to visit at the end of the month as we planned? I may need your help with fundraiser ideas!

Jay

Biiiiitch

How are the boys? Are they delicious or what?

Give me the deets. STAT love u

Me

Haha, I love you. Still deciding about the boys. I haven't seen any under the age of 50. I will keep you posted. I'm going to some town fair tonight. Wish me luck.

I saw the three dots appear instantly, and then it stopped. I threw my phone on the bed and opened my suitcase to find what I could wear to the fair. After 45 minutes of looking in the mirror at every possible outfit combination I brought, I settled on a gray and white striped t-shirt dress. It cuffed my body nicely. I wore my knee-length socks and combat boots. I pulled my hair out of my space buns, and they fell into perfect light curls. Makeup isn't typically my style, but I threw some on anyway. I stood and looked in the mirror at myself, and I smiled. *Damn. I look good.* I pick up my phone and see the time. 6:10 pm I grab the last bits of my sandwich and eat it in one big bite before reading my text messages.

Mila

FaceTime me whenever you're free. We need to catch....

Jay

Oh, giiiirl, call me later, don't care wha.......

Maybe: Nancy
Hey Olive! Call me xo.

I unlocked my phone and checked Nancy's text message. I could get back to my friends later. After one ring, she answered.

"Heyyyyyyyy. Where are you? My girls and I want to go hang out. I told them about you, and they can't wait to meet you too." She already sounded tipsy. I knew this would be a bad idea, but I was here for the summer and survived better with friends and socialization, so I needed to try this.

"Hey, yeah, I'm staying at Elora Inn. You can come here unless you want me to meet you at the fair; I'm just finishing up and need to have a drink before I go," I replied nervously and chuckled.

"Be there soon!" Nancy hung up excitedly.
I fixed myself in the mirror and talked to myself.

You are fine. You're fine. Just mingle, and you can come home.

A few minutes passed before I heard a knock at my door and instantly knew it was Nancy because they were fast little knocks. I listened to the laughter coming from beyond the door. I pulled it open, and there she was with her two friends. All of them dressed similarly—all gorgeous, perfect barbie dolls. One of them stood out, though. She was beautiful. But not in an 'I love myself' kinda way, natural beauty, effortless.

"You look ahhhmazing!" Nancy shouted. "This is Lynn" she pointed to the left of her, and there stood this tall goddess with beautiful black coils and brown sugar skin. She vibrated with good energy. "This is Katrina." She pointed to the right of her: brunette hair, way too much makeup and an all-around snobby vibe. I hadn't spoken to her and knew I didn't like her. Nancy pushed past me and walked inside; her friends followed. Katrina scrunched her nose and shot me with *'I don't like you either'* eyes.

"Hey, you're new here, right? So nice to meet you." Lynn put her hand out to shake mine and smiled. I liked her.

"Hey! Yeah, I'm just here for the summer doing an internship with Coral Reef." I replied,

"Wow, that's awesome. We *have* to hang out." Lynn smiled.

"LETS DRINK BITCHES!" Katrina yelled as she pulled a bottle of vodka from her purse and took a big swig. She handed it to Nancy, who did the same. Next, Lynn shimmied toward them and grabbed the bottle, she then looked toward me and shrugged with a smile, so I took the bottle and joined them. What can go wrong, right?

We sat in my room listening to music, and the other girls had to touch up their makeup before we could leave, so I tried to fit in by asking them average girl conversation questions.

"Ugh, I just love Gabe!" Katrina blurts as she reapplies her pink-shaded lipstick. Lynn just laughed, but the entire room went silent when she did.

"What?" Katrina grunted. Nancy's eyed just sat widened, her jaw on the floor. Like she was shocked, someone would cross Katrina.

"You've been dating for like a month. Relax," Lynn complained.

"You don't know shit Lynn; you're just jealous because you've been single your entire life." She scolded.

"Okay, break it up, ladies. Pause this until later. We have somewhere to be. Agreed?" Nancy chimed in at the perfect time, and to my luck, it worked, and wc headed for the door. No more words were spoken until we arrived, and the energy had shifted even then.

♦ ♦ ♦

Chapter 2: The Trauma

Present

Agnus looks toward me with concern and anticipation, all in one. “So, what happened, Dear Olive?” She sits there across from me. Her arms were on the table, and her fingers twined, listening closely to what I was saying.

I’m not used to this openness with my friends and family, let alone a total stranger. I mean, they know the important stuff, but I guess the authentic raw details, their mine- and now, hers. I’m doing this solely because this decision is essential, and clearly, I can’t make it alone, or I would have already. Why is it so hard?

“Do you need a break?” Agnus asks.

“No…uh, I’m okay. But this next part is dark. Are you sure you want to hear it?” I uttered.

“Honey, I’m 71 years old. This old thang has seen quite a lot in her lifetime,” she replied.

I chuckle. “Okay, okay. Shall we go for a walk?”

“Let's do it. Should we find a bench in High Park?” Agnus stands up, puts her jacket, hat and scarf on, then slides her hands into her pocket and pulls out her gloves. She starts walking toward the door, and I look back; I don't see Doreen, so I put money on the table for my coffee and follow Agnus. It's only about a five-minute walk to High Park.

"So, you mentioned your husband passed away last year. Do you have any other family in the area?" I curiously ask, trying to divert the conversation from myself for a while.

"Well, yes, I do." Her eyes open wide, and she smiles from cheek to cheek. "I have two children who are much grown now. With a daughter and a son, I have five beautiful grandchildren who live just a few hours out of town. I see them as much as I can."

"That's sweet. I'm sure your family appreciates it. What keeps you out here if they are there?"

"Well, you see, my husband… he loved the city. We moved here decades ago, and my heart won't let me leave. This place…" She motions her hand around toward the park and the city surrounding us. "It's home." She smiled, but this time it was a familiar, cheerful smile. We find a bench and take a seat.

"Ready when you are. Take your time." Agnus nudges me with her elbow and raises an eyebrow. "You don't have to speak about it, though, if it's too hard."

"It's fine. I just needed a second.."

Past

After about an hour of listening to music and pre-drinking, we made our way to the harbourfront, which was jam-packed with people. Drunk people at that. Most of the day leading to the night had me feeling anxious, but once the alcohol set in, my mood changed, and I found myself swaying to the music playing in the distance; I was laughing even at the boring jokes being told, and I was having a great time. I picked up my phone and dialled Mila; she didn't answer, so I just left a cute sweet voicemail,

Listen, Milaaaaa, bitch. You're supposed to pick up the phone!! What are you doing, screwwwwing Wyat?? Muah, love you bye

Next, I scroll drunkenly through my phone to find Jay's contact, but now I'm stumbling, and my phone looks like it's got a twin. I sit back down on the bench and take a breather. I had forgotten I was even going to call Jay because the alcohol had done its job, and I no longer felt anxiety while partying with those strangers. I was feeling myself, and the cute boy with blue eyes and blonde hair was staring at me from across the lot. So I had the nerve to walk up to him and say hi.

I stepped down from the bleachers, and as I approached him, I could feel my face get warm and my cheeks turn red. This happens to me whenever I get nervous. Even though it was getting late, it was summer, so In the distance, I could see the last bit of the sunset on the horizon. The light breeze swept past me as I got closer to the strange boy who seemed to mesmerize me. I smelled the fresh-cut grass as I stumbled, almost missing the moment to catch myself before I fell. As I righted myself, I blurted out, “Hey. You’re cute.”

“Well, so are you. What are you up to tonight?” The stranger replied and took a step closer to me.

“I just got into town today. I’m here for the summer doing an internship.” The alcohol had worked a little too well because I found myself pushing my lips toward his within minutes of our first conversation. I didn’t care about who he was or what his story was. I just wanted a distraction, and with the alcohol flowing through my veins giving me that warm feeling, it made everything spin. I didn't care. Hours passed, and I learned he was also an out-of-towner, only here for the weekend — staying with his cousin. His name was Blake. His cousin was Nate, who was born and raised in Elora. Our groups had combined, and things were going smoothly. Our lips intertwined, and everyone else was gone when we stopped to breathe. The girls went off with whoever and left me alone. But I felt safe until…… until i didn't.

"Care for a walk?" Blake smirked at me.

"Sure, why not?" I replied. Something in my bones was telling me, pulling at me not to go, but I dismissed it as a wave of drunken haze flowing through my veins, so I grabbed his hand and stumbled off the bleachers we had been sitting on. It was dark, and I suddenly realized how drunk I was once I had started walking. Everything was spinning. The cool air danced on my cheeks; Mine and Blake's hands were still linked, and I tried hard to see where I was walking, so I didn't fall. I could tell we were walking through some field, but in the background, I could hear the noises of the party happening around us. I wanted to ask where we were going, but my spinning head kept commanding my heavy legs to trude forwards. Fireworks started going off and lit up the sky. I stopped, sat in the grass, and looked at the sky. "I need to sit down for a minute." I blurt out, not asking, but stating.

"Sure." Blake sits next to me and puts his arm around me.

For a minute, things were amicable. Then I felt a warm rush of his breathe against my face as he started slowly kissing my neck, cheek, and then he slithered his way to my lips with his arm still around me and the other draped over my legs. We have a rhythm going, or at least that's what my drunken brain convinced me. I knew in a few short moments I would be over this, I almost felt bad for not wanting to go further. I straightened my back and began to slowly pull myself away, just as my lips part from his I manage to escape an "I can't" under my breathe but the devilish grin on his face tells me he thinks otherwise. In the next moment, he pushes his lips back on mine and I endulge him for a second longer before pulling away for a second time, with a little more force. He tightens his grip around my legs and I look up at the clear sky, pleading. I hear the sounds of his belt buckle, I can see him shimmy out of his jeans using his one free hand while holding my drunken, limp-like body in place with his other. Next thing I know, his pants are at his ankles, and he's yanked my dress up and shoved my panties to the side; I must have blacked out for a few seconds because the next thing I remember is feeling cold and dry between my legs, followed by a hard, painful, deep thrust of him sliding himself inside me. I let out a yelp. It took me a few moments to realize what was happening. My hands gripped the grass as he pushed himself inside me harder and faster with each thrust. I focused on the grass; it was cool, slightly damp and freshly cut. After what felt like an eternity, I came to enough to squeak out.

"Stop. I don't want to do this."

But He doesn't stop. Instead he lets out a hiss, almost as if he enjoyed how much I wasn't enjoying it. I felt sick.

"Stop. Please."

At that moment, the distant sounds of all the people at the carnival fading into the background and seeing the look on the face of this evil being towering on top of my body, his sly, serpent-like smile, made my blood start boiling to the point where I had a surge of adrenaline. I pushed him off me, got to my knees, and started crawling away. He pulled me back.

"It's fine. I won't be long." He let out a little laugh, and I caught him licking his lips. He grabbed my ankle, and I reached out for anything to grip onto. I felt his rough, calloused hand pull me closer, and he forced himself into me again. 'No.' I thought as I gathered all my strength in my tiny body, and I turned around and smacked him with all my force.

"Get the fuck off me!" I screamed. Loud.

I looked over and saw people walking past us, it was so dark they couldn't see us, and it was so loud nobody heard my cries.

"Fuck. Sorry." He stood up and pulled his pants up.

I jumped to my feet and pulled my dress down, trying to adjust. I turned around so I didn't have to look at this monster a second longer. I started to panic. I wanted to run but knew my head couldn't match my legs. I was too drunk and had no idea where I even was. I felt gross. I felt used. I felt disposable.

He took a step forward and grabbed my arm.

"You were into it. You teased me all night."

I felt his warm breath, shivering down my neck. "Fuck you!" I shouted, and I went to push him away, but I was so drunk that I stumbled backwards.

♦ ♦ ♦

Chapter 3: The Aftermath

Present

I stand up off the bench and pace back and forth. "I've never told anyone that before." I blurt out.

"Oh, Olive. I'm so sorry that happened to you." Agnus stands and puts her hand on my shoulder.

"It's okay."

"It is absolutely not okay, Dear. I'm sorry that you had to go through something like that. Boys these days just aren't bred the same." She scuffs. "Don't get me wrong; I know this happens no matter what decade it is. But why has it become so common? I watched my talk shows, and they spoke on this numerous times. They had feedback and callers from the audience… Anyway, it's tragic." Agnus is talking fast; you can tell she has no idea what to say to me. "What happened next?" We sat back down on the bench.

The hard part is over.

"That was how that day became the worst day of my life. But it also became the best day of my life, from what happens next."

Past

Before he can grab me tighter, I spin to turn around and notice a shadow come out of nowhere and tackle him. But that can't be right, can it? I see Blake being mauled by this shadow of a tall man. I can't see anything else. I stand there and watch, unable to speak or move. After several minutes of Blake getting only half of what he deserved, this tall figure stands up and spits down at him. "That's what you get, you piece of shit. Leave town and never come back, or you won't be able to walk away next time." He turns to me with panic in his eyes.

"Holy fuck. Are you okay? I mean, of course, you're not okay. Please let me help you. Do you live close?" He reaches out to grab me and begins scanning my body. "Are you hurt?"

"I… I…thank you." I start to sob uncontrollably. I go up to this stranger and hug him after what happened. Something tells me if he was willing to save me, he wouldn't hurt me. "I'm drunk, and I need to lay down."

"Where are you staying? Let me get you home?" He insists,

"Elora Inn." I try to point in the direction of where it is, but I have zero ideas where I am right now. I start zigzagging across the grass when this guy comes behind me.

"Here, let me help you." He puts his arm around my back to hold me steadily. Walking to the motel felt like miles away because everything wouldn't stop spinning. I saw a girl come out of nowhere, but she seemed to know this guy.

"Is she okay? What happened?"

"No, she's not okay. Help me get her back?"

"Of course."

When we finally make it back, he looks at me and back at the motel. "Which one?" I pull out my key and hand it to him.

"I know which one." It took me a second to realize it was Lynn from earlier, one of Nancy's nice friends. There was a tag that read 12 on it. He led me to the room and unlocked the door; I stumbled into the room and left the door open. I immediately fell onto the bed and started to quiver as I sobbed into the sheets. He walked into the room, and so did Lynn, he shut the door and asked Lynn to help me get out of my clothes, but I refused. After what felt like an endless amount of time, she gave up and left, and I fell asleep in the clothes I had been wearing, and when I woke up throughout the night, it had been dark still, and this guy had been sitting on the floor, he stood to his feet immediately and rushed toward me softly.

"Hey, I'm sorry I didn't get there quicker, but you're okay now. That guy won't be coming back." He said, and I could tell, even with all the alcohol I had consumed, that he meant it. "My name's Carter, by the way. Are you new here?" He asked.

"Olive..." I tried to get the words out. "I'm here for the summer."

"Well, Olive. I will sit here until you wake up to ensure you are okay, alright?" He found a spot on the ground and got comfortable. I dozed off. When I woke up, I stared at the ceiling for several minutes and thought of how much my head ached.

For a brief second, I forgot what happened the previous night until I looked over and saw this tall, strange, beautiful brunette man sitting on the floor, leaning against the bed and having one of my books open on his chest; it was Jane Eyre. He fell asleep, so I tried not to wake him as I sat on the bed and groaned instantly. My head hurt. All the memories flowed back slowly, and I wanted to sob. I wanted to scream. I jolted off the bed, aimed for the floor, ran as fast as possible into the bathroom, slammed the door shut, and locked it.

I looked at myself in the mirror and barely recognized what I saw. My once favourite sweater was now a reminder of what had happened to me. The makeup running down my face indicated that I was crying a lot. Anger started to travel through me, and I began to strip. I pulled the sweater over my head and tossed it onto the floor. Next, I pulled my socks off and threw them, too; I took them off anything that had been on me, throwing them in each direction. I heard a frantic knock at the door.

“Are you okay?” Carter asked,

“No, I’m not. You can go. Please.” I replied.

“Can you just come out for a second, and then I'll leave?” He insisted, so I ripped it off like a bandaid, opened the door and stepped out. I was in my bra and underwear; frankly, I didn’t care. His eyes didn’t even wander to my body for a second. They just stared into my eyes with such genuine concern. I looked away, walked past him, and grabbed my gray track pants and the first t-shirt I saw, a plain black one. “Listen, thank you for everything you did for me. You don't need to do this, though.” I waved my hand back and forth between us.

“Do what?” He sounded confused.

“This whole being nice to the wounded girl thing you got going on. I’m fine. It’s my fault. I shouldn't have been drinking so much or initiated it first.” I sighed, sat on the bed, and wished this encounter would end. I was embarrassed beyond belief seeing Carter in the daylight, realizing just how well-proportioned his body was and how he towered over me, with loose curls in his chestnut brown hair that fell over one side of his face. He had a rugged look to him, but it was attractive. I pushed the thoughts away, wishing to erase the last 24 hours and start over.

"I may not know you, but I know it wasn't your fault, so please don't think like that. Before I go, I just wanted to let you know if you need anyone to talk to - I'm here. I live in town. You're working at Elora Reef this summer, right? I work there from time to time with maintenance. Ronnie told me we had a newcomer named Olive. Anyway, I'm here. I wrote my number down on the paper over the dresser. Don't hesitate to use it." Carter walked toward the door and opened it. "It was nice meeting you, even under these circumstances." And he walked away.

Whoa. I don't know what to think, but I hope I never have to face anyone from that night again. Although I know that's wishful thinking.

Present

"So, this guy, Carter. He is who you are strung up on? Why are you getting drunk, wandering alone in the streets at night, and sleeping on subway benches.... What happened? You say that it was also the best day of your life. Is it because of him?" Agnus is talking a mile a minute. "Oh, sweetheart, the trauma must have been difficult to deal with." She scoots over and puts an arm around my back to my shoulder.

"Thanks, Agnus. It's okay, though." I give her a *thank you* nod. "I pushed past it pretty fast and fell into things with Carter. I focused on work, too. He healed me, and I don't regret anything because it led me to him saving me and bringing me home safely. I had seen him several times since I started work, but we spoke no words for weeks. We just nodded our heads and smiled." Remembering my past brings up these old memories I prefer not to think about; I go on anyway. "I was grieving everything in my way and embarrassed by what had happened. All I did was work, go home, cuddle up to my blanket, watch TV, and eat as many snacks as possible before I got sick of sugar consumption and fell asleep."

"Dear, when I was your age, things like this occurred all of the time. Although I never experienced quite what you did- my sister did. We were sixteen when it happened, and she was on her way from school. I was at home that day because I was only a year older and was already caught up on my schoolwork. I spent the day sleeping and doing absolutely nothing. My poor sister, Darlene - was on her way home, walking alone, when she was attacked from behind, assaulted and left on the road to die. She managed to crawl back home, but it was so late when she did, and everyone had already been looking for her." I wince in pain. How awful that must have been for her sister. I'm fortunate that Carter was there to save me from further damage. "Darlene wouldn't talk about it for months and hid in her bedroom all day and night. Healing from the internal and physical wounds that incident has caused her." Agnus wipes the tears from her eyes with her hand and sniffles.

"The world can be a cruel place, can't it?" I say, comforting her.

"It sure can be, but you know what, Olive? It can also be beautiful. Keep going with your story if you're ready." Agnus says,

Past

It took days for that numb feeling to sink in and for me to start feeling the withdrawn and enraged stage of it all. I've heard about it in the movies and TV shows. The victim falls apart, they lose themselves, and I felt sad and broken for weeks, but not like this. I think I'm more than broken. I spent the day pacing back and forth around my room, trying to fight my thoughts, telling me to pack my things up and just leave. This was the tell-all sign that this wasn't my fate, that this job was a bad idea.

I came up with a plan, and I'll go home. I'll tell Mom it wasn't a proper fit and that I want to spend the summer at home. I'll let her know I'll get a job and do whatever she wants if she doesn't question me further on my decision to return home.

I told myself to scrap that plan, to run to Jay's or Mila's and convince them to let me stay with them all summer, hiding out - I could lie to Mom and tell her that everything is excellent in Elora, but just be slugging it at my friend's house. Drowning in my sorrows.

I spent the day coming up with hundreds of plans to escape this one I'm living in, but before I knew it, it was dark outside, and I'd spent the day fighting with myself. I put on Gilmore Girls and cuddled up in bed.

I'm running through a forest, and I can't tell where I am because there's so much fog blocking my view. I don't know who I'm running from, but I feel terror through my entire body. I slow down, but I don't ever stop. I look behind, all around me, looking for something, for someone. My fingertips are frozen, and the tip of my nose is too. I start screaming, pick up my pace, and then trip over a rock, smashing my face into the ground. I taste the dirt in my mouth and pull myself back up, but when I do, I get pulled back; when I turn my head, it's Blake. 'Leave me alone!'

I awoke in a panic and felt like I couldn't breathe; I gripped my sheets, then slapped my chest, trying to bring myself back to reality. When I could catch my breath, I told myself;

Breathe in, breathe out, you're okay, you're here.

I could taste salt on my lips, and my sheets felt wet. I was drenched in sweat. I hopped out of bed and paced around the room.

I need to leave, and I have to get out of this place.

No, you don't. You're strong; stick it out.

All this place has brought me is fear and sadness. I can't stay.

You can do this, Olive.

The internal battle with myself continued for minutes; I rushed into the shower and changed my clothes. Without thinking, I pack my bags, tossing anything and everything into my suitcases. I didn't slow down for a second; I threw my belongings into the trunk of my car and drove off. I had no intention of returning.

The drive back home was fast because I left in the middle of the night, and by the time I arrived at Jay's doorstep, it was 5:12 am. I used my key and tried to sneak into his apartment without waking him, but when I stepped inside, It was so dark I couldn't see, so I knocked a ceramic owl on the floor, and it shattered, sending sounds echoing through his thin apartment walls. I hear Jay's footsteps when they get out of bed, tip-toeing to the door.

"I have a weapon, bitch!" He shouts, swinging a bat toward me as he opens his door.

"Holy fuck! Jay, it's me, Olive." I grab the bat and push him away, "Seriously? Jesus."

"What are you doing here, Olive? It's almost 5:30 am; you're supposed to be in Elora. What's going on?" I fall to my knees and start to howl out tears; I don't stop, I can't breathe, and Jay drops to the floor with me. He spoons me in a big hug and rubs my back,

"It's going to be okay, Ol. You're safe here; I've got you." After an hour, he stands up and leads me to his kitchen, down his slim hallway, and we sit at his table. He doesn't pull out coffee. He pulls out Vodka, orange juice, and two cups.

It takes me hours to get out of what happened, between the tears from both Jay and me. There were moments Jay wanted to speed race to Elora and '*find that fucker,*' he said. But by lunchtime the next day, we had made it to his basement- living room area, where we fell asleep watching my 600lb life. When I awoke hours later, Jay convinced me to go back. He told me that he'd be there to visit me in the next week or so.

"I'll facetime you every damn hour if you need it, Ol. Remember why you did this. You need it. Don't let one terrible memory taint this place for you." Many tears were shed in the less than 24 hours I had been at Jay's house.

Nonetheless, I mustered up the courage to get off Jay's couch, move my two little feet and make it to my car. I drove back to Elora - broken, a shell of a person, less of who I was before this happened, but I made it. It was Sunday night, and I was ready to sleep and bury myself in work.

Chapter 4: The First Day

I didn't get much sleep the night I arrived back in Elora. My mind had been racing, I was talking myself into staying. I told myself,

Jay will be here soon; hang in there until then.

Jay has always been my comfort person. Mila is my best friend and my soul sister. She and I will never not be in each other's lives. Jay is my everything. Life wouldn't be the same if he upped and left my life. They are the two most important people in my life.

The first thing I looked for when opening my eyes, at 6 am - was coffee. Thankfully I had a kettle and instant coffee here, so I didn't have to venture out for it. I sat on the edge of my bed for a long time, it felt like hours, but it was only minutes, twenty to be exact. I splashed water on my face and didn't even bother to put makeup on. My skin has been clearer lately, so I haven't been messing with it. I brushed my messy loose waves into a tight low bun, then pulled a few side pieces out to frame my face. I found my plain pink crop top and black high-waisted slackers with my white converse. On the way out the door, I grabbed my coffee, the extra one I had made to go, a slice of pre-packaged banana bread from my mini-fridge and my blue jean jacket.

I wasn't ready to face this, but the truth was - I had no choice. The walk felt nearly impossible; I felt like pulling my foot out of drying cement with every step, fighting internally with myself. With every other step, my brain screamed to turn back, but my body kept trudging.

I got there in ten minutes, dragging my feet the whole way.

I can do this.

I walked up the steps, entered the building to my new workplace, and took a deep breath. "You're late." Nancy declared in a snooty tone.

"It's 8:03…." I said,

"Yes, you start at 8." She added

"Cool. Where do I start?" Nancy rolled her eyes and walked toward the door, entering the other area of the Aquarium, motioning me to follow her. She hardly spoke to me, and I couldn't determine her deal.

"Do you have a problem with me?" I blurted out. Nancy spun around to look at me,

"I think you're a drama queen, and getting Carter to *'save the day'* like that was just unnecessary; Lynne told us what happened, and just so you know, Carter and I kind of have a thing." She said it in a tone as though she was trying to convince herself.

"Do you even know the first thing about what happened?" I'm fighting back tears, but in no world was I about to let this little bitch bully me over the assault she knew nothing about. "I'm just here to work. Where do I start?"

"Whatever," she said, rolling her eyes, "Ronnie wants you to change the water temperatures to the sea horse enclosure; three degrees colder- we're putting new fish in there, taking the seahorses out," She said, but something about it felt sly. Still, I was in no mood to argue with her, and she had no idea how hard it was for me to get out of bed this morning.

Without even giving me direction, she stormed off. Leaving negative energy in the room with her. I brush it off and figure out where to start myself. Seahorses - colder. Got it. When I enter the back room, it's pretty easy. It's just a nozzle. I got close and started to scan every button.

"Whatcha doin' there?" Carter comes from behind me

"Oh, just turning the temperature down for these guys."

“Whoa, don’t do that. It’ll freeze them out.” He steps in front of me, blocking the buttons.

“Seriously? Nancy, she told me to… So, you do have a thing, then? Is that why she has it out for me?” I scuffed, annoyed.

“No. It’s not like that.”

“Then what's it like?” I hesitate, but I need to know.

“It’s like this; we had a fling long ago. We were kids; she was probably twelve, me thirteen. She always wanted more and pushed for it even as we got older- but it didn’t feel right to me. She’s my sister's friend, that’s all. But still, she finds a way to slide into my relationships. A new woman comes into my life, and she sabotages it. I’m sorry.”

“But why me?” I asked, confused.

“Because she’s insensitive and doesn’t think before she acts. Again, I am sorry, Olive. How are you doing?”

“I’m as good as expected. Can you give me real direction regarding work? Where’s Ronnie?” I tried to change the subject.

“I’m unsure where he is, but let me show you around. Give you the basics until he can let you know more.”

Carter introduced me to the animals at the Aquarium; he showed me how to feed them and what to watch out for. We went into detail on adequately cleaning the tanks and keeping them as natural as possible. He told me how to watch for algae and other signs of diseases or cracks in the tanks. After an entire day's worth of cleaning, I got to leave. Carter had already left, but Nancy sat at the desk when I left.

"Thanks, by the way," I said as I walked past the desk. She was always just sitting on her phone when I saw her.

"I don't care what your problem is with me, but If I catch you putting these animals at risk again, you will regret it. Mark my words." I walked past her, not giving her a chance to reply. I was done with the day.

When I walked outside, It was raining.

Great. Just fucking great.

I didn't have a hood, because I only brought my jean jacket. So I put my phone into my pocket and planned to run back to the Inn. I wasn't going back inside to sit it out with Nancy. Just as I reached the end of the steps, Carter came rushing around the corner.

"Come with me!" He shouted, behind the sound of the rain smacking against the pavement. I followed him to what seemed to be his car. "Get in;

I'll drive you " I hesitated but got in any way; he saved me already, and there was no way he'd put me in harm's way now. I close the car door to the passenger seat of his Deep blue Jeep. It was tidy like it had been for a new detail.

"So, how was your first official day?" Carter smiled as he started the car.

"Oh, you know, minus this crazy girl that works there, you might know her, her name is Nancy, and she's obsessed with this good-looking guy who works there as well," I teased.

"You think I'm good-looking?" He raised an eyebrow as if he didn't know how good-looking he was. I playfully nudged his arm. The drive to the Inn was all of two minutes,

"Can I walk you inside?" he asked; he was very gentlemanly. I'd love to meet the woman who raised such a God of a man.

"Thanks, but I think I can manage" I smiled and waved as I exited the car. I watched as he drove off. Some of me wanted him to come inside with me for some reason.

The rest of the week at work was slow, and Carter had not made any more appearances, which I was slightly disappointed over. Nancy earned her daily remarks whenever we crossed paths, but by the third day, I was over it and ignored her altogether. As it was getting closer to the end of the week, I knew Jay would be coming soon, and for the first time since I'd been back, I was looking forward to something.

♦ ♦ ♦

Chapter 5: The Friendship

Jay has been my best friend since grade four. I was the geeky kid nobody wanted to hang out with, and Jay was always hidden in the shadows; nobody made fun of him, but he didn't have many friends. Luckily enough, he picked me to befriend. We've been best friends ever since.

Jay's story is, we'll say — complex. He's gone through way too much shit in his lifetime. He's one of 3 kids; his twin brothers Rock and Todd, are typical dudes. What I mean by that is 6'5, built, jocks, brains. Jay was always considered the 'weird' brother at home. He had always been compared to his identical twin brothers, the handsome Gibson twin brothers. He was always different, which made him the most wonderful person I know. He told me he was gay when we were 17, and it never changed a thing. I respected him for coming out and telling the world just how great he was. His father was a total dick bag. Being gay wasn't good enough for his family, and he would tell him repeatedly that he was 'sick' and he could send him somewhere to get help. His mom stood by and let the abuse happen, but she never let him send her son away. His brothers, in my opinion, were dip shits, but they always seemed to have Jay's back even when they teased him constantly. He spent a lot of time at my house. He is my soulmate, in a platonic way.

So when Jay arrived, short of a week after I had returned - I was more than excited to have a familiar face joining me, and he was staying with me for nearly two weeks. I pulled his suitcase and bags inside and shut the door. "I'm seriously so excited you are here. You don't understand." I admired his sweet face and lifted an eyebrow, looking as he pulled little Red out. We piled into the bathroom and turned the fan on, letting all our stress slip away while I hot-box the bathroom.

"I'm sorry about what happened to you, Ol. How are you?" Jay was leaning against the wall, eyes barely open but completely alert.

"It's okay, Jay. I'll be fine. You survived it, didn't you? I can too." Jay went through something similar years ago when we were in our last year of high school. It was hard for him, but he made it through after therapy and many movie nights.

Jay and I had this routine of taking over our bathrooms and hot boxing them. At his childhood house, he had a bathroom in the basement, which was rarely used. I would tease him about it because it was a massive Jacuzzi tub that was never used.

We sat inside the dry tub, smoked, and talked for hours.

I found myself lying in the dry bathtub at the Inn, staring up into nothingness, letting the high take me away.

"Doesn't make it okay. Let's go out! Maybe we'll stumble into Sir Savior?" Jay always knows how to turn something negative into something positive, and it's one of my favourite qualities about him. I rolled my eyes and scuffed.

"I can't move, not yet, anyway," I said

—

By the time we got motivated, the high was gone; we got dolled up and headed out. We had no plan other than to smoke our pains away and wander the streets of Elora. I was never much of a smoker, but when Jay was around, we bonded over it. It was our thing, even though he was a full-time stoner.

We stopped to take selfies and photos of each other as usual. We had come across the University of Elora, which was old and looked haunted. Jay made us take selfies outside of it when he proceeded to pretend to lick the statues out front. The walk felt like miles because I had to pee as soon as I left the Inn, but I wasn't going back. We headed for the harbour so I could try to get over my fear of the trauma. Hand-in-hand with my best friend. As we approached, my eyes searched for the bathrooms, and to the right of me, I saw a small group of guys, and to my surprise, I saw Carter with two of his friends, and laughter echoed. I nudged Jay, and whispered,

"That's him!" and ran for the bathroom. "Be right back!" I couldn't hold it anymore.

I don't think Jay will ever fully admit what was said when I went to the bathroom, but I know Jay, and he probably was much more vocal than he'll admit. He may be tall and skinny, but he's fierce. He said it went a little like this;

Jay

Standing outside waiting for this bitch to use the bathroom, I couldn't help but feel the urge to walk over to him and see his deal. He saved her and then didn't say shit after the fact. Is he being heroic or ridiculous? Maybe a bit of both. But he kept my best friend safe, so I needed to thank him, and his friend was cute and gave me this look that said he wanted a piece. So I headed toward the group of guys.

"Carter?" I asked. He stepped forward.

"That would be me." He said curiously,

"I'm Jay, Olive's best friend. Can I talk to you?" I took a few steps back and waited for him to follow. "I have to say this quickly before she gets back and plots my death. Thank you for doing that. To save her."

Carter grunts. "Uh, yeah, I'm just sorry I didn't get there a few minutes sooner. How is she doing? Is she okay?" He rubbed the back of his neck with his hand nervously.

"She's tougher than she looks. I wouldn't waste time, though. If you are into her, you better show it." Olive walked out, and when her eyes reached mine and saw what was happening, she stopped dead in her tracks and laughed.

"Seriously, Jay?" She approached us and then stopped next to me. "Sorry about my friend and anything he may have said to you." Her eyes squinted toward my way, and she gave me the "fuck you" look.

—

Olive

I didn't know it then, but that horrible night was also the best night of my life because I had met him. After seeing him with Jay, things quickly changed between us. Our love story began on the night of July 1st at Elora's Canada Day carnival.

The morning came quickly, and I headed to the aquarium for the day. I had the fundraiser idea to run past Ronnie and thought it could significantly make an impact in saving the aquarium. We could set up a booth, hand out flyers and give people a look inside what we do with short presentations. I wanted to get to work early so I didn't miss Ronnie. When I arrived, I slid into our conversation that we could run a booth at the carnival. I told him I already spoke with the town spokespeople and there was a spot for him. I was glad he agreed, and last night while I couldn't sleep - I gathered up supplies and made a banner that said 'Elora Reef.' I painted it for hours; until it was complete with little figures of animals surrounding the words. I made it colourful so that it would pop.

"Here" I pulled the sign out that had been rolled up. "I made this. I hope it's okay."

"That's fantastic! Thanks, Olive. It means the world to me." Ronnie smiled hugely, and when he did, I noticed that he had a lovely smile. I didn't expect it because the way he dressed was, instead, scruffy - like appearance didn't mean much to him.

The day went by quickly, and every time I passed Nancy at the desk, she would look up at me and scuff. Since our last interaction, she has backed chiefly off, but her energy is worth a million words. I still needed to understand her problem.

Jay spent his days relaxing and hanging out with Little Red. He said he goes for walks, but something told me he was hiding something, so I saved it in my mental notes for later. I entered the building, went to the back room where the lockers were, and pulled out my work shirt to throw over the top. Our work t-shirts were basic, navy blue collared shirts with a small Reef logo on the left side of the chest with the words, 'Coral Reef' on the back.

"Hey." I heard the deep voice out of nowhere, and I gasped.

"Holy shit! You scared me." I sighed and started laughing, relieved it wasn't a serial killer with an axe and that it was Carter looking fine as usual,

"Sorry." He said. "I wanted to ask you something. Are you going to the carnival tonight? I was hoping we could hang out." He said, fearful of my response. I could see it in his eyes.

"Yeah, I'm going. We've got a fundraiser booth set up for Elora Reef. I would love to meet up." A beam of joy radiated through my body, and I felt my cheeks redden being in his presence. I assumed he wasn't interested this entire time because I was the poor wounded girl he saved on my first day in town. I guess I was very wrong. I wouldn't deny the chance to check him out for myself.

After my shift ended, I went to exit the building and noticed Carter out front sitting on the steps waiting for someone. He turned around and stood up as I walked down the steps.

"Hey, I just wanted to check. Did you want me to pick you up or meet you there?"

"Jay and I can meet you there. He's coming too, is that all right? I didn't even think to mention it earlier. He's in town for a few weeks." I took a deep breath because I was feeling guilty.

"No, it's no problem at all. I'll be with my friends for a bit too, Ace and Gabe. I would love to introduce you." He walked down the steps and turned back toward me. "I'll see you around seven, then?"

"I have your number; I'll text you." I waved as he left. I watched his big frame walk away until he disappeared. I think I spent most of that time picturing him undressing.

It was approaching closing time, and I was exhausted. I wanted to return to the Inn and relax for a few hours. I couldn't find Ronnie, and Nancy wasn't in her usual spot. So, I head for the door and exit the building with my jacket and purse in hand.

I stop dead in my tracks when I see Carter talking to Nancy just ten feet away. His back is turned to me, but Nancy was facing my direction. They looked to have been in a serious conversation, so I didn't move. Nancy leaned into Carter and gripped his arm with her hand; she quickly glanced in my direction - sending me a sly smile and shivers up my spine. It felt malicious.

Nancy didn't know me, though. She didn't know that I don't take that shit. I stomped down the steps and stormed past them, giving Nancy an evil eye.

"Olive! Hey, wait." I realized at that moment that Nancy hated me because she knew that Carter and I had bonded while I was there. Because she was in love with him.

My stomach was hurting, but I kept walking. Carter rushed behind me, catching up quickly. I didn't hear him say anything to Nancy. He just left. Part of that made me happy. "Wait up! Olive?" He stopped in front of me. "You okay?" He sounded concerned, and it made my heart feel all types of ways.

"Didn't want to interrupt your conversation with the Wicked Witch, that's all." I let out a whine; I had my arms crossed and my stance strong.

"Wicked Witch?" He laughed. "You're funny, Olive. And I didn't want to converse with her. She just has personal space issues. I was waiting for you." He stepped closer to me, and my arms fell. "You're adorable when you're jealous."

"I'm not jealous!" I shouted, then I wandered my eyes around, realizing how loud I was. "I'm not," I added. As luck would have it, I started walking, and he followed behind me.

"Okay, fine. You're not jealous." He admitted. Putting his arms up, in surrender mode. "But if you were, you should know - I do not like Nancy." Carter looked in my direction, and I could see it from the corner of my eye, but I didn't give him the satisfaction of showing how happy that statement made me. We were close to the Inn now, so I slowed to a stop and turned my body to his;

"Okay," I said, smiling so ever slightly.

"Okay." He said, smiling back at me.

"I'll see you later, then?" He asked me,

"Yeah." I smiled and walked away.

When I got in the door, Jay had been awaiting my arrival. He could tell right away something had changed in my demeanor. He raised an eyebrow and started to smile.

"What happened? Why do you look so giddy?"

"Well, Carter talked to me today…." I paused.

"OK, and?" Jay stood up, walked toward Little Red, grabbed her, and handed her to me.

“He asked me to ‘hang out’ at the carnival tonight.” I grabbed Little Red and squeezed her, and warmed her up.

“Yes, bitch! You should wear that plaid skirt with the white sweater crop top you wore to that fall festival we went to last summer. It’s perfect. Did you bring it? What about the white ankle boots or brown hat?” Jay loved when I let him pick out my outfits, so I didn’t stop him when he interfered.

We spent hours that felt like days, tearing up our suitcases with questionable fashion possibilities and trying things on until we finally decided on high-waisted dark blue jeans and a purple-toned cropped sweater. I even added a necklace for some flare.

Jay picks dark blue ripped jeans and an oversized nude blue sweatshirt with an ACDC logo on it - even though he doesn’t know one song by them. He pairs it with a Y2K choker and a teddy bear backpack. He’s a fashion icon.

I glanced at the screen of my phone and noticed the time; 6:45 pm. So I unlocked my screen, searched for Carter's number, and texted him.

Me

Hey, it's Olive. I’m going to help Ronnie out now. I’ll text you when I’m done.

Carter

Sounds good; talk soon

♦ ♦ ♦

Chapter 6 The Carnival

Jay and I walked down the street, and from afar, we saw the sky light up in the distance. The carnival lights were coming from the rides. As we got closer, I noticed the Ferris wheel and heard the screams from the lifts. There was a cotton candy booth, hot dog stands, anything you wanted, name it, and I bet it was there.

"I'm nervous. I need to get to my booth and check on Ronnie" I wiped the sweat from my palms onto my jeans and took a few deep breaths.

"It's fine, O. What do you have to lose? He's hot and into you. You're here for the summer. You might as well have fun. What's wrong with a little summa lovin'? Go work, then get your butt back here!" He winked and nudged me on the shoulder. "Maybe I'll even find myself a little snacky poo tonight." We started to approach the entrance, and it was swarmed with people. Jay tried to direct me to the rides, but I stopped,

"I'll meet you in an hour. I promised I'd help out." I rolled my eyes and shrugged, then walked off. Time passed quickly; I handed out flyers and smiled at everyone approaching. We raised a decent amount of money within the hour I worked,

"Go wander; come back before closing. Thanks, Olive." Ronnie said,

"Thanks." and I wandered to find Jay.

I found him a few minutes later; I just followed the skunky smell until I saw him hunched over in a corner. "Let's go, stoner." I pulled at his arm until he started walking with me.

"Fine, party-pooper. How was it?" He asked.

"It was… alright. What were you up to?" I scold Jay with my suspicious eyes.

"This, drama queen." He lifted his hand and pointed to his joint.

"Mhmm." I link my left arm to his right, and we walk together until we're closer to the entrance.

I scanned everyone until I saw Carter standing with one hand in his pocket and the other running through his hair. He was laughing with two guys, who I assumed were Ace and Gabe. "There they are! Let's go!" Jay smiled, and Gabe nudged Carter. When he turned and saw me walking toward him, he coughed, pulled his hand out of his pocket, and took a few steps toward me until we met halfway.

"Hi." I couldn't help but blush every time that sweet smile and deep aqua eyes stared into mine. I just wanted to know what he thought when he looked at me. Did he feel this energy between us that I thought? I lifted my arms, wrapped them tightly around his neck, and held the hug longer than I should have. Jay came behind me and slapped my ass, pushing me into Carter and causing us to crash. I regained my balance, and we pulled away once we realized how close we had gotten.

“Let’s go bitches. You have time for that later. I need a hot dog.” He winked at me, walked ahead of everyone, spun around, opened his arms big, and looked up at all the twinkle lights hanging around us. “I just love carnivals!” he shouted. I love Jay; he brightens up every room he's in. I ran toward him, put an arm around his shoulder, and touched my head to his as we admired all the lights hanging around us. We turned around, and all three boys stood there, hands in their pockets, keeping quiet and letting us do our thing. Once we had had our moment, we let go and walked toward them.

“Sorry, Hi! I’m Olive.” I said, extending my hand to shake theirs.

“I’m Jay,” he said with that magical smile of his, the one that made many straight men question their sexuality.

“This is Ace, " Carter pointed to the red-headed heartthrob to his left. He nodded and smiled, “and this is Gabe." Gabe was tall, rugged and covered in tattoos that peeked out from beneath the collar of his shirt.

"Hey, nice to meet you both." He put his hand out and shook Jay's hand; he looked back and smirked in my direction. Then pulled me in for a quick awkward hug. Ace stood there awkwardly, like he was not used to this situation. We made our way into the carnival as a group.

"Where to first?" Carter asked; he looked into my eyes with a sweet embrace.

"I kind of want some Cotton Candy." I shyly said.

"Cotton Candy? Let's do it. C'mon, boys!" He hollered, and they walked ahead of us to the line for the cotton candy stand, which was only about ten feet from where we were standing.

"Ok, I'm telling you, that guy is gay," Jay whispered and looked toward Gabe.

"Seriously?" I looked over to the boys, who were all deep in a conversation, and I tried to see what he saw, but Jay said I don't have an excellent 'gaydar,' so to me, I saw a dude named Gabe. As we conversed, three girls approached the boys, and I realized it was the girls from the first night here, Nancy, Katrina and Lynn. Katrina jumped onto Gabe and wrapped her legs around his waist.

"Baby! There you are. I was looking for you everywhere." She said, and he put her back on the ground. I glanced over at Jay and gave him the 'guess you were wrong' eyes.

“Uhh. Yeah, sorry. I forgot.” He scratched the back of his head, and then she looked intently toward us. The colour from Jay’s face leaves within seconds, and my heart hurts for him. I may be shy, but I get uncomfortable when my friend is not feeling great. And when I’m uncomfortable, I have a big mouth.

What happened to me the night I was with them was awful. She ignored what was happening and left me alone with a stranger. I hate them all. Fuck them, and fuck this.

“What is *she* doing here?” Katrina said the word ‘she’ like I was some fucking poison. Carter turned around with the tray of cotton candy in his hand and realized what was unfolding, his smile dropped to a frown, and he picked up his pace to join the group.

“Stop,” Gabe said, and he looked pissed. “Let’s just go.” He added, grabbing Katrina’s arm and trying to walk away.

“No, why is she here?” Katrina looked angry but in that annoying bitch kind of way. Instead of speaking like a normal human, she whines like a toddler, making me hate her even more.

“Do you have a problem with me?” I shouted and stepped forward, ready for a fight, and Jay looked at me like he wasn’t prepared for angry Olive. I didn’t care, though. I wasn’t about to be bullied by a barbie monster all summer. Nancy whispered something, and before Katrina could step forward, Lynn grabbed her arm, and Katrina pulled back.

“Don’t fucking touch me.” She hissed at Lynn. “My problem is I don’t like you. You come into our town acting like you’re better than us with your stuck-up attitude.” She looked toward me and had one finger pointed at me like a total Karen. I laughed.

“I *am* better than you, sweetheart,” I said. She tried to take another step toward me, but Carter intervened before she could. Even though I could tell, he held back a smirk from how I snapped back at her. “Lynn, get your annoying fucking friends out of here.” Carter looked at her and yelled and then motioned his hand to her. “Seriously, get out of here.” He added.

“Whatever, let's go.” She said, but mouthed, *‘i’m sorry.’* She seemed stressed but grabbed both her friends and linked arms between them. “Let’s go on the Ferris wheel,” Nancy shouts.

“Woooo,” Nancy seemed like she was already wasted and not even in the same world as we were. She leaned into Katrina, whispering before she looked back to give me an eye roll and then walked away. As soon as she turned her head, I wrinkled my nose in disgust and looked over to Jay, silently standing there watching everything unfold. I only noticed that he had pulled out a joint and lit it up without a care.

“Bitches.” I mumbled under my breath, thinking nobody heard me. Jay looked at me and said,

“Gonna smoke this and walk, so it’s not so obvious. I’ll catch up. Before I do, let’s get a picture of this! The lighting is perfect.” Fucking Jay is always making things so awkward. He positioned us in front of the cotton candy booth, aimed the camera up so you could see the neon sign, and said, “Ok, say ‘cotton candy’ and hold it up!” There! Perfect, ok, I’ll see you soon, he walked off before letting me question him.

“Uh… Anyway, this has been ‘eventful’ so far. What’s next?” and then smiled, so Carter knew I was being playful, “You know those awful girls?” I asked him hesitantly.

“Lynn is my sister…Yeah, I know. How can she be my sister, right? I'm white as a ghost, and she's got beautiful tanned skin, yadda, yadda - I’ve heard it all. She’s my half-sister. We have different dads.” He started munching his cotton candy, and we walked together through the carnival.

“So, your sister, huh?” After that encounter, I tossed the remainder of the cotton candy into the trash bin, realizing I wasn’t all that hungry.

“Yeah, she’s cool when she's not hanging out with the other two. The problem is that there are few people in our town to hang out with, and she just got familiar and comfortable with them. They've been friends since they were little, but Katrina especially is brutal to deal with." He tossed his cotton candy into the next trash bin we saw, only a few feet away from the last one, and turned to me. "Look, I know how you feel about them, and I don't plan on hanging around them, okay? If they try to bother you at all, tell me." We took a few steps and stopped in front of the Ferris wheel. "Shall we?" He winked and opened his arm for me to join him, so I linked my arm to his and walked toward the Ferris Wheel entry. I prayed that mean girls had moved on and we wouldn't see them again.

"Thank you."

"For what?" He stopped and turned toward me.

"For just being nice to me, listening to me when I talk," I said.

"It's my honour, madam." He joked as we climbed into our cart. When I stepped in, the cart rocked, and my head spun. Carter grabbed my waist to help me steady. I couldn't tell if I was lightheaded from the ride or the jolt that went through my body as he touched me. The ride started to move, and I gripped my hands on the seat while my heart started to race, as it does when I do anything slightly scary.

“Confession?” I turned my head slowly and looked at him. “I hate heights.” I let out a fake laugh, and he looked down as the ride started moving, realizing it was too late to get off.

“Why didn’t you say anything?” Our cart started to swing, and my eyes shot open, closed, and opened again. I didn’t know what to do.

“Don’t look down!” Carter laughed loud when he saw me slide close to him and grab onto him when our cart stopped at the top.

“What's happening? Oh my god, are we stuck on this thing?” My head hurts.

“No, we’re okay. They’re just letting people on the ride.” He replied. “Come here.” He wrapped his arm around my shoulder, and I cuddled up to his neck.

The thing is, when someone tells you not to look down, you’re going to look down. When I did, I noticed Jay in the distance. He was hiding slightly behind a wall; I only saw it was him because his Teddy backpack had a keychain dangling from it, and it was shining, giving him away. He wasn’t alone; I could see him with someone else, a man. Taller than him and with a bigger build, I couldn’t tell who it was, but they were close enough to tell me it was an overly friendly interaction.

We spent the next hour together, going on rides and playing all the games we passed by. Carter even won me a stuffed Penguin toy.

"I love Penguins. Thank you." I said to him, smiling from ear to ear. "I haven't smiled this much in a long time. My cheeks hurt." I stopped walking and stood in front of him and took a step closer, and suddenly the feeling of my beating heart was vibrating through my entire body.

"My grams also loves Penguins." He smiled at me.

"Your grams' sounds pretty cool," I added, winking at him playfully.

"I like you, Olive." He said, and his fingers slowly grazed mine. He stepped an inch closer, so close that our bodies were touching, and I could smell the cotton candy on his breath. He grabbed my hand and pulled it toward his chest and then put my hand where his heart was. "Do you feel that?" he held his hand over mine, touching his beating heart for longer than I could admit. "I'm not sure why I feel the way I do, but I know my heart only beats this fast when you're around me." He whispered into my ear.

I shyly let out a giggle and pulled my left hand up. Even though being this close to him made me feel heavy, I pulled it up, placed it on his neck, and looked into his eyes. Their blue tones shine brightly from the lights surrounding us, staring into mine. That stare was speaking a thousand words as he said,

I know you feel it too, Olive.

We didn't need to talk, we just stood there looking into each other's eyes, and then I leaned my forehead into him, and he bent down a little until he reached my height and placed his forehead on mine. I sigh with relief. I opened my eyes, and my lips moved to match his, and then…

Present

"And then what? What's with the delay? You can't just leave me hanging here, Dear." Agnus shouts. I laugh.

"I'm hungry," I say, and then I stand up and escort her to walk out of the park. "My apartment is down the street. Let's have tea and sandwiches." She nods, and we head to my apartment. It takes about 8 minutes because I've taken this route many times in the last two years I've lived here. We enter my apartment, and I realize what a total mess I've let it become. I started to panic mildly and apologized numerous times before she said,

"Oh, dear, please don't worry about it." She shrugs and walks toward my kitchen like she's been here before. "So, how long has it been since you've seen this Carter boy?" Agnus walks around my kitchen, carefully examining things and where they are placed, she pulls out the kettle, fills it, and then pushes the button down. She finds the mugs and then places them next to one another. She pulls two out and puts one into each cup. It's still odd how normal this all feels.

"Don't get ahead of yourself. Before we get to that part, there's much more to the story." I sigh, remove my coat, and place it over one of the four chairs around a small rectangular table. I glance over to Agnus and smile. "Thank you for listening to me, Agnus." I genuinely mean it; it's nice to have a fresh perspective; as I said, I'm desperate. I know what to do, but my heart and head love to play tricks on me.

"I must say, Olive, I enjoy myself and your company. I would rather be here listening to your story than riding the bus just for the sake of leaving my house. Let me make the sandwiches. You go freshen up." She opens my fridge and takes everything out to make them. I walk away, head for the bedroom, and shut the door behind me.

For the first time today, I want to cry. I miss him. Sometimes when I'm walking down a crowded street in Toronto, I think I see him for a second, and then he's gone. I brush the sad feelings off, remembering I have a random sweet old lady sitting in my kitchen awaiting the rest of my story. I grab fresh clothes, brush my hair, and throw it into a bun. I wash my face, brush my teeth, and return to the kitchen. Before I join Agnus, I turn my phone on silent and plug it into the charger behind the end table in my living room.

Walking into the kitchen, I see Agnus sitting at the table, reading the newspaper. So I sat down and joined her. We eat in peace and sip on our teas. She was giving me space, but after ten minutes, she said, "So, what's next?" I smirk, take another sip of my tea, and then place my hands on the cup and rest it on the table.

Past

"Ugh, Carter! Where the fuck is Gabe?" Katrina came out of nowhere, with her followers towing behind her like little ducklings, evil ones ruining our perfect moment.

"No idea. I thought he was with you?" I sensed the frustration coming from him because we were about to share our first kiss when this annoying twat came out of nowhere to ruin the moment, typical.

"No, he left right after we walked away. He said he went looking for you. Ace left and said he had something he had to do." She looked concerned but also confused, and I couldn't care less. He was probably hiding from her.

"Let's go look for him." I looked up at Carter, grabbed his hand to show him it was okay, and smiled. "I need to find Jay anyway." He smiled, and we started to walk toward the exit. Katrina followed behind us with Nancy and Lynn.

"Where the fuck did he go?" Katrina's anger was getting more prominent, and her horns were about to emerge. Before we knew it, Gabe stumbled out from a dark shadow and immediately grabbed Katrina's arm.

"Let's fucking go." He started to drag her toward the exit, and you could hear screaming in the distance, but I couldn't determine what they were saying. Lynn looked over toward Carter and grabbed Nancy. "I'm going to get her home, okay? I'll see you later?" She looked panicked as she dragged her wasted friend home.

"Um… Okay then, what was that about?" confused as ever, you could tell Carter felt the same as I did.

“Good question.” He said, and his forehead wrinkled like he had no idea what had just happened. Jay stumbled out of nowhere minutes later, approaching us from behind.

“Biiitch, I need to go to sleep.” He grabbed me and put an arm around me so I could help him walk. Something was off, though. We saw Nancy trying to run off and Lynn attempting to catch her and bring her home. I could tell Carter wanted to help his sister, but he felt terrible leaving me.

“Go help her. The motel is right down the street. I need to get Jay back anyway. Text me, okay?” I grabbed him with my free arm, gave him a side hug, and then he ran toward his sister. Then they ran around in circles as Nancy dodged them, laughing her ass off.

“GO, SISTA!” Jay yelled and punched his fist into the air. We walked back to the motel, and I plopped him onto the bed and took his shoes off. I grabbed a water bottle and placed it beside the bed on the end table.

“What happened tonight, Jay?” I nudged him, but he was barely awake. I didn’t know where he got the alcohol from, but he wasn’t drunk before he walked off, that I knew. He didn’t answer me and instead just slurred words and groaned. I finally made out part of what he was saying, and it was something like this,

"He's... heeesssaa queer... uknowwhatImeanNn " No, I do not, but I ignored it and let him sleep. I'd save my follow-up questions for the next day. That night, all I wanted to do was wash my face, throw my hair up and get comfy. So that's exactly what I did.

I went to the bathroom and shut the door, letting Jay silently sleep off his drunk. I hopped into the shower, quickly washing my hair, face and body. It only took me a few minutes; when I shut the water off, I heard Jay yelling,

"So what, you have a fucking girlfriend?" He slurs his words, but I can tell by his tone he's beginning to sober up.

"Fuck you, don't tell me you care, not after tonight." I hear a noise, sounding like Jay's phone bouncing off the wall. I wait ten minutes before exiting the bathroom, and when I do - he's fast asleep, snoring.

When I returned to the bed, I sat down and grabbed my phone, and my heart skipped a beat when I saw Carter's name. It said he texted me 15 prior. Shit! I unlocked my phone and opened his text message.

"Come outside?"

I panicked and grabbed my sweater, and pulled the door open. There Carter stood, leaning against a post. His hand grazed his hair, and he turned around when he heard the door open. I was embarrassed because I looked like a hot mess. If he had come twenty minutes earlier, I would've still been all done up. I was wearing the bottom of-the-barrel clothes because they're my most comfy. I tried to cover myself, doing a terrible job, and he giggled when he saw the panic on my face.

"Don't worry. You look cute."

"Thank you." I took a step outside and quietly shut the door.

"Nancy made it home okay, and Lynn?" I asked.

"Yep. Everyone's good."

"Cool." I stood there awkwardly, unsure of what to say or do next. It went silent for a minute before we both tried to talk simultaneously, overlapping our words.

"You go first," I exclaimed.

"I didn't want to leave like that. We had a moment back there, and it got ruined by the Katrina-Gabe drama. I also can't get you out of my head." He took a step forward and grinned. My stomach was flipping, and my fingertips went numb, but my legs and lips moved faster before I could back out. Once they reached him, we moved slowly, deeply. His hand moved to the back of my head, gripping his fingers through my hair, and the other moved down to my waist, pulling us close. I could taste the cotton candy on his tongue as we moved in sync. It was passionate but soft. He ran his fingers down my spine, giving me a shiver. Before things got too heated, our kiss ended, and we pulled away.

"Wow." He said. "Now I can go to bed peacefully, Olive Chambers." He grabbed my hand and kissed the top of it, and then walked away. I stood there for a few minutes and found my finger stroking my lips, the spot where he had just been.

I got inside and immediately pulled my phone out and FaceTimed Mila. She needed to know everything. We talked for hours while Jay snored beside me, sleeping off his drunk. Mila was worried about me after what had just happened to me. She didn't want me throwing myself into some random stranger in this town. She's always been the logical one, always stood by my side.

"Please just be careful, Ol." She said as she sat on her bed painting her toenails while she spoke to me.

"I know what you're doing. Thank you, and I love you, but it'll be okay. You'll get to meet Carter when you come to visit. Where's Wyatt?" I asked, but the camera is constantly freezing up on one of our ends, so FaceTime was and always will be a constant annoyance. We still participate in it because it's our way to communicate best since we're far away from each other this summer.

"I'm here!" I hear him yell in the background. She looks over at him and smiles.

"Okay, I better go. Love you guys, bye!" I hung up before she had the chance to respond. I needed sleep.

♦ ♦ ♦

Chapter 7: The Family Boat

The following day came fast. Luckily for me, I hadn't been drinking. Since my first night there, I had stayed away from it. On the other hand, Jay had become best friends with the toilet all morning. I figured I'd wait until he felt better to question him about the previous night and fill him in on the kiss. The kiss that I couldn't seem to forget. It was so sensual and gentle. It had real emotion, and I wasn't sure I had ever been kissed like that before, how Carter kissed me then.

My first kiss was with Andy Stevens, I was in grade five, and he was in grade six. Our school had these annual fairs to kick off summer; we'd spend the day playing games set up all around our school and the soccer fields around us. Normally, I'd walk around with Mila and waste time. That year, though, Mila had been sick, so she was home; I found myself sitting alone on the steps for the first hour. Andy came up to me, and he was this boy whom I always smiled at but never spoke to. I was young and very timid. He approached me with one of his guy friends and asked if I wanted to spend the day with him. Nervous but excited, I said yes. He held my hand and brought me an ice cream cone sponsored by our school.

Nonetheless, these small gestures set me up for high expectations for years to come. It was the last half hour before school ended and summer kicked off; I knew I'd never see Andy again, he was older than me, and we had nothing in common but the smiles we shared throughout the hallways. We walked up to the hill before the soccer field, found a spot, and sat down. He told me about his interests, how he loved Hockey and hoped to make it big one day. Before I got up to leave, he told me, "Olive, you're pretty cool." He leaned over and gave me a juicy peck on the lips and then hugged me. "Have a great summer," he said as he walked away. I never did speak to him again, and honestly - I didn't think about him until many years later. I thought, "*Why can't every moment be that special?"*

After hours of Jay hovering over the toilet bowl, he emerged from the bathroom and found a spot on the bed. "Ugh, my head hurts." He groaned and covered his face with a pillow.

"Do you remember anything from last night?" I asked. I stood up and gathered all my toiletries from my suitcase and pulled out jean shorts and a tee.

"Yes, vaguely. Why?" He pulled the pillow from his face, looked at me, and raised an eyebrow. He sat up, grabbed the water bottle from the bedside table, and chugged it back in one swig.

"Just curious where you went off to all that time, is all. Also, Carter kissed me." I took a step forward and grinned. I couldn't help how I felt when I admitted it for the first time. We kissed, and I felt so much from it.

"Wait, what? You KISSED?!? I'm happy for you, babe." He winked and turned toward me in the bed. "I need food."

"Give me 5." I went for a quick shower, and once I stepped in, I realized how hungry I was because my stomach was angry and letting me know. Before entering the shower, I stood in front of the mirror, admiring myself. The light in the bathroom shined on me perfectly.

My hips were slightly wide, and I stood 5ft, 3 inches high. My pale skin was shining, and my stomach was bloated, but I loved my body. I even loved the birthmark shaped like a square on my hip. I had comfort in knowing that my assaulter hadn't seen me in the nude. I zoned out with the water shooting down my back, and it took much longer than expected because I couldn't get my mind off of Carter. I took my time lathering my hair in shampoo. It's the only one I ever use, and it smells like peaches, and I refused to use anything else. I shaved my lady bits and my legs. Just as I went to lift my leg, Jay pounded on the door,

“Hurry up bitch!” I sensed anger in his tone, but I gave him a break because he drank a lot last night, which wasn’t normal for him, and I thought something else had happened, but he wouldn’t tell me what it was. I went to turn my body and slipped backwards, grabbing the shower curtain that surprisingly held me up, but in the process, I dropped the razor and got a cut down my leg just below my knee. Drip. Drip. All I saw was the blood running down from my leg before everything went blank, and the next thing I knew, Jay was hovering over me. “Holy fuck. Are you okay?” I panicked, realizing the state I was in, so I tried to get up, but all I felt was pounding on my head and throbbing in my leg. I couldn’t move. I shut my eyes, and when I opened them, I was lying on the bed, covered in a blanket.

“What happened?” I sat up and still felt the pounding in my head.

“Cover those babies up.” Jay turned around and covered his eyes seconds later, I realized my boobs were on display, and when I sat up, the blanket covering me had fallen.

“Oops.” I laughed. Jay isn’t too fond of female body parts.

“Well, the damage on the cut is small, but you bleed easily. How does your head feel? You’re such a weak bitch, Ol, it's barely any blood, and you passed out. Sheesh." Jay says, shrugging his shoulders.

I stood up slowly, holding onto the end table on my way up. Once I was sure I was stable, I took a few steps toward my suitcase, grabbed underwear and my white and blue striped short romper, and put it on swiftly. I looked down at my leg and noticed it was covered in bandages, so Jay must've had quite the time between being hungover and dragging my naked body over to the bed and then having to clean up my wounds and bandage me up. It made me laugh trying to picture it.

"That was traumatizing, Ollie. I had to drag your naked, wet, bloodied body through the room and plop your ass onto the bed. I almost grabbed your phone to call your lover boy to help me." My heart raced thinking of the embarrassment I would've felt if he had done that.

"You wouldn't have" I shot a death stare his way and wrinkled my nose in disgust. "I hate you," Jay smirked.

"So, are you good?" He asked. He handed Little Red to me and a bottle of Tylenol.

"This should help." I enjoyed Little Red before grabbing my bottled water and popping two pills. The fall was more embarrassing than anything. I had a tiny bump on the back of my head and wasn't sure of the size of the cut, which seemed like it was for the best at that moment. Blood and I don't mix too well.

We headed down the street to the nearest diner, where we found ourselves in our regular booth. I was expected to spend much time buying food since I had moved there just for the summer. I didn't see the point in renting a place. I had a small kitchenette in the motel, but it was nothing special. I didn't mind spending time at the diner because it allowed me to observe the town's people, which became a fascinating hobby of mine. People there were built differently than people in Toronto. They were friendly and caring, everyone smiled, and I wasn't being pushed around by people on the sidewalks. It was peaceful. I noticed other people who had routines that included dining at Franny's.

For instance, this bald older man with the cutest beagle would be by the diner every morning and night. He would get coffee and a donut in the mornings, and at night he would stroll past. I often wondered if he had been alone with his dog. He seemed happy, so I never questioned it. His dog followed his slow pace as he wandered the streets, letting the dog sniff every post or tree he saw.

There was a group of teenagers who would be loud and rowdy, and they'd laugh and joke around. There never seemed to be any issues. It was just a fun group of kids who would spend all their time hanging out. I liked that. There was a family of 5 who would come in on weekends and have dinner together. I thought it was sweet. I picked these things up because it's who I am, but mostly because I just wanted to know more about that strange little town.

After flipping through the menus, I decided on the cheese and ham omelet, and Jay decided on the bacon, eggs, and toast combo. We both got large coffees, and once we had several moments to digest the coffee, I broke the silence. “So tell me what happened.” He knew what I was discussing, but getting Jay to discuss things was impossible. I have to shake it out of him, and it’s frustrating beyond belief. He shifted in his seat like he was uncomfortable but sat up straight and placed his coffee mug on the table.

“What do you mean?” He grabbed his phone out of his pocket and unlocked it, pretending to keep busy. I placed my hand over his phone and pushed it down.

“Tell me. What’s going on?”

“I met someone.” He ran his hand through his hair. “Uhh. He's ‘straight,’” He said sheepishly.

“Okay, so, you like this guy?” I asked. Typically, Jay prefers quick hookups and doesn’t tend to stick around long.

"Kind of. I don't want to, though. He's a mess, and it's not like I'm exactly here to stay. I like him, though."

"Who is it?"

"It doesn't matter. I'll let you know if it is anything, but I don't think so, Ollie." I changed the subject because it seemed to change his mood drastically, and that's not what he's here for. We made plans to head to the market after this and grab a few things for the week to munch on and anything we could shove into our little fridge. I wouldn't say it's a 'mini,' but it's not a regular-sized one, definitely not big enough for more than one person, but we can make it work. We paid our bill and made our way through the front doors. When we reached the sidewalk, Jay stiffened up.

"What's up?" I looked over and noticed Carter's friend, Gabe and his girlfriend, Katrina.

"I don't like her." He says,

"That makes two of us." I'm not lying either; she's horrible.

"Listen, I'm going to run to the motel and grab a little puff, and my head is still killing me. I'll meet you at the store." He walked away, and I went in the opposite direction, toward the market. I came to love that town. I took my time and took the long route to the market, which only added a few minutes, but that way, I got to walk past the harbour and explore the town better as I thought of what to grab at the store and to give Jay some time before we met. I passed by the spots Jay, and I took photos the day he arrived, and it put a smile on my face.

When I approached the harbour, I stopped and leaned on the railing, looking out onto the water. I saw boats upon boats, families coming and going. It was a lovely day, so I soaked up the sun and felt the wind on my face, legs and arms. It felt nice, almost surreal. The breeze was incredible on a hot day and was the perfect temperature. I opened my eyes and watched the birds fly in the sky, landing to grab food and take off again. I looked to my right and noticed someone waving at me in the distance. I squinted and covered half of my face with my hand because the sun was beaming down on me, making it hard to see in that direction.

It was Carter. My stomach started flipping, and I tried to hold back my excitement when he walked toward me. I stood straight and took a few steps toward him until we met halfway. “Hi.” I smiled. I felt my cheeks going red, so I turned my head away for a second and talked myself into playing it cool.

“Hey there, beautiful.” He stepped close to me and grabbed my hands, facing straight on. He leaned down and kissed the side of my head. He left me speechless because I didn’t reply until he spoke again. “You okay there, Olive?” He smirked. He could tell it was more of a ‘holy shit, and he kissed me’ type of way and not a ‘new why did he do that’ speechless.

“Yes, sorry.” I grabbed him and reached for a hug. I loved how his hugs felt. He wrapped his arms around my waist, and we fit perfectly together. I pulled back and looked at him,

“What are you up to?”

“See that boat over there?” He pointed to the beautiful party cruiser boat with a nice sitting area and what looked to be a cabin built in as well. I saw an older male and female and two younger kids. “I was having lunch with my mom and dad and my two sisters. Want to join?” There was no way I wanted to meet anyone in his family. We had just met.

“I better not. I’m going to meet Jay at the market.” Plus, I'm also not ready to be around anyone's parents. I barely like speaking on my own.

“Can I walk you there? I was finishing up anyway.”

“I would love that.” He ran over to his family's boat and then headed my way. He grabbed my hand instantly and started walking down the path.

“Is this okay?” He lifted our linked hands and glanced toward them.

"Yeah, It is." I meant that. I was never one for affection and PDA, but something about this small town and Carter made me want to do things I never did before. It's mostly quiet, but not in the wrong way. We enjoyed silence and nature as we walked down the path. We approched the market, and I stopped and unlinked our hands.

"Thanks, Carter"

"Can I ask you something?"

"Absolutely."

"Can I take you on a date?" I couldn't contain my excitement; I'm sure my face showed it. I didn't even care that work had been in the back of my mind since I started there, but I couldn't get too attached to the place. I was there for the summer, so I offered a helping hand during my time there, and I needed to take it as it was. I still needed to approach Ronnie about the fundraiser idea. I had already written out a plan for it.

"I mean… of course. I would love that. Where would we go?"

"I'll see you tonight, 7 pm. I'll pick you up." He leaned in and kissed my cheek again, with such a sweet embrace and gave me a gentle hug and then looked back and smiled before walking away. Great, I would need to prep in less than 7 hours. Jay didn't show up to the market, but I wasn't too concerned because that is typical of Jay. He hated food shopping and would leave it to me most of the time, so I grabbed our regulars and returned to the motel. When I entered, Jay wasn't anywhere to be found, but the lingering smell of Little Red showed he had been here not too long ago. I turned my music up loud and started tearing through my suitcase to find the perfect outfit. I dug through dresses, skirts, and rompers but decided on high-waisted jean bell bottoms with slight knee rips and a white crop top. I put it on the bed and headed for the shower. I've always liked to take my time getting ready, which meant I'd be in the shower until the water turned cold.

As I was mid-shower, I heard the door creak open and shuffle, so I knew Jay was finally back from wherever he went. I took my sweet ass time until my skin went cold, and I hopped out of the shower. I placed a small towel over my head and another around my body.

Jay was sitting on the bed with his laptop and TV, watching RuPaul. He looked up at me. "What's with the mess?"

"I'm going on a date," I said with a slight squeal because I was so excited. I gathered the clothes I had laid across one side of the bed and scooped them into my arms while still holding my towel intact. I heard vibrations when I looked over and saw Mom pop up on my screen. I looked back toward Jay.

"You're not going to answer that?"

"I'll call her back later."

"So, where are you going?" Jay grabbed his laptop, placed it in his lap, and started scrolling, keeping his attention on me.

"I have zero ideas. Carter said it was a surprise. What are you going to do tonight?" I walked to the bathroom but left the door open to still hear him, but I didn't need to traumatize him with my lady bits, especially since the last shower incident.

"I'll probably catch up on emails and Netflix. Order in." I walked out of the bathroom, stood there, and stared at Jay.

"This ok?" I asked.

"I would add that cute bright pink cropped cardigan overtop and button it up. Always looks cute on you." I bent down, grabbed it, put it on, and then stood in front of the tall body mirror that hung on the wall in the bedroom area.

"You're not wrong." I grabbed my curling iron and makeup bag and sat in front of the mirror because it was low enough to the ground, and I could also see better if I sat on the floor. Hours went by, and my hair and makeup were finally done. It was 6 pm. I had time to kill before Carter picked me up, so I sat next to Jay and peeped into his FaceTime call with Mila.

She reminded me she would visit sometime next month for a weekend trip. We caught up on life since the last time we spoke, aka the previous night, and the next thing I knew, I heard a knock at the door. I stood up, grabbed my phone, and shoved it into my back pocket. I took one last glance in the mirror and was pleased with my appearance. “Kay, later, love you, mwah.” I blew Jay and Mila a kiss and walked out the door. I shut it behind me and turned around to see Carter standing with his hands behind his back. He had black straight-cut jeans, a white t-shirt, and a button-up gray shirt over the top. He had a thin coat over top of that and smelt so good. He smiled the brightest smile, pulled his hands from behind his back, and had a single rose.

“A single rose for a beautiful lady.”

Present

“Are you sure you want to hear more?” I ask; Agnus has made herself comfortable between the pillows on my couch.

“Don’t stop on my account. I'm invested now. I need to stick it out until the end.” I lean on the other end of my sectional couch and prop some pillows under my arm.

"Okay, so the date." I continue before I hear a loud knock at my door, but they're loud, fast knocks, which means it's Mila. She lives one floor up with Wyatt in their apartment, but we spend a lot of time with each other when we can or just come to each other when we need things.

"Olive," she yells, "Open up! I need to borrow some milk. I'm trying to make cupcakes to bring to Wyatt's parent's house, and I need milk!" She keeps knocking, so I stand up.

"Sorry." I look toward Agnus. She stands up and walks toward the bathroom down the hallway.

"Don't worry about me, Dear. I'll be right back."

"Coming, stop fucking pounding on my door like a maniac." I unlock the door and open it, and she bursts in.

"What took you so long?" She walks toward my kitchen and opens my fridge, pushing things around until she finds my milk, and then she takes the carton.

"Sorry, I'm tired. I had a rough night."

"You know, we'll have to talk about how you were a no-show to see him yesterday. It's not healthy to hold it in." Mila goes in for a side hug while juggling my milk carton and her phone in one hand. I hug her and then walk toward my door in silence. I'm just not ready to tell her about it, then it becomes all too real, and I'm trying to deal with it on my own. Before I break the silence, she does it for me,

"I'm sorry, Ol. I know it's a sensitive subject, but I worry about you. Anyway, wish me luck. Call me later?" She walks out the door, and before I shut it, I yell,

"I love you." And then I shut my door, returned to the couch, and waited for Agnus to return.

"You didn't have to hide in the bathroom; it was just my best friend, Mila," I told her. She sits in the spot across from me like she was before.

"I didn't want to intrude. It's no problem." She smiles, places her hand under her chin, rests on it, and motions me to continue.

Past

He bowed a gentlemanly bow and opened his arm for me to link mine to his. "Where to, Sir?" I got nice and close, and he guided the way. Not many people drove in Elora because everything was within walking distance. I headed for the street leading to the central part of town.

"Are you hungry?" he asked me.

"Starved."

“We better hurry then!” We walked to the harbour, and as we got closer, I realized he was taking me to his boat. By that time, the sun was setting. Once we got to the gate that allowed you to get to the docks, he asked me to close my eyes, and I obliged.

“Don’t let me fall.”

“I would never.” I could feel the wobbling of the docks with each step. Once we stopped, I assumed we were out front of the boat, but I didn’t open my eyes yet. “Stay there. Don’t move.” I heard the water rocking under the boat as he stepped onto it and shuffled around before I saw the sky had become lighter underneath my eyelids, but when he said, “Okay, open your eyes.” I opened them and saw the boat was filled with twinkling lights. I gasped. It was beautiful. The sun was setting, and the boat felt like we were straight out of a rom-com. He grabbed my hand and led me onto the boat. When we turned the corner, I noticed he had filled the front seating area with many blankets and pillows. The table had two plates with a big tray covered by a lid. I saw just how big the boat was. It had an outdoor sitting area and a little living room on one end.

“This is….” I was speechless. Nobody had ever done anything like that for me before.

"You did all of this?" I stood there, dumbfounded. The poor guy put so much work into it, and I was standing there awkwardly.

"Yeah, do you like it?" His smile was so contagious because once he looked into my eyes with that beaming smile, I couldn't help but smile too.

"I love it." My eyes started to swell with tears.

"What's wrong?"

"It's just that nobody has ever done anything this nice for me before." I sat on the bench seat wrapped around the table with a mysterious platter.

"Well, I'm glad you like it. You deserve this and so much more. Can I give you a tour?" Carter put his hand out for me to grab, then led me inside the boat. Which, to my surprise, was also a lot bigger on the inside, like the Tardis. It was beautiful and modern on the inside. A small kitchenette, a table with two bench seats on each side, and a small bedroom and bathroom broke off into each direction. He walked toward the other end of the boat, where a small spiral staircase led up to a small deck on top and where you operated the boat. He pointed to the seat, motioning me to sit down as he started it up and took off. "We're not going far, but I wanted to show you something." The ride was only about 5 minutes, but I didn't go on boats often, so I focused on the waves making little ripples in the water. The way it sounded sloshing around, smacking against the boat, was so calming. Once we stopped, he grabbed my hands. “You look beautiful. Have I told you that yet tonight?”

Gosh. This man complimented me like no other. “Have I told *you* that you look beautiful tonight because holy fuck?” I said and then pressed my fingers together and kissed them. “Perfecto.” I could tell he wasn’t used to that sort of affection or forwardness from women because his eyes widened, and his cheeks went rosy, and I liked that more than I should have.

I stepped forward, placed my hands on his neck, and pulled him closer to me. Before any second guesses, I pressed my lips onto him and then his hand slid down my back, slowly reaching my ass and firmly squeezing it. His moans as we kissed could have made me break out into a thousand orgasms right there. I pulled away for a second, and the lust in his eyes for me made my legs weak, his lips so swollen, and within seconds he pushed his face back onto mine for a few minutes before we mutually stopped and pulled away. I hugged him tightly, he pulled me onto him, and I wrapped my legs around his waist. He spun slowly and let out a sigh.’

Present

"Are you still with us, Dear?" Agnus shouts.

Damn. I start using my hand as a fan to wave myself off. Thinking of these intense sexual moments with Carter reminds me of how long it's been since I've had sex.

"Sorry." I can feel the heat rise in my cheeks, showing I'm now blushing. "Let me continue. Sorry." I add.

Agnus just giggles, understanding I got lost in the moment.

"So, he told you that you looked beautiful, and then what happened?" Agnus, she's so sweet and so invested in the story. Note to self; no more getting sidetracked by my hormones.

Past

"You make me feel things, Olive," Carter said. I didn't reply, I just hugged him tighter, and he pulled me in as close as he could and lowered his head so it was closer to mine, as he's 6ft and I'm 5'5. Even though I couldn't see his face, I could tell he was smiling and that he knew I was too.

"I have something for you."

“Is it what’s under that shiny platter down there?” I smirked. He started to walk away but didn’t lower me to the ground. Instead, when I tried to squirm away and smack him, he didn’t budge, so I started to laugh, and he kept me wrapped around him.

“Put me down!” I started to smack his back again playfully. “You’re going to break something going down those steps!”

“Ha ha.” Before I could escape, we made our way down the steps safely and backed out on the deck, and then he lowered me and took a bow.

“For you, m’lady.” He gestured for me to sit, so I sat down and waited for him to pull it open, and when he did, I immediately began to laugh.

“How did you know?” I looked up at him but covered my mouth with my hand and continued laughing. It was a platter of tacos, my favourite food.

“I may have seen Jay and asked him your favourite food, to which he told me, ‘the girl loves her tacos.’ So, Taco’s it is.” He walked off, and when he returned, he had two sodas. “He also told me you had a weakness for Root beer, and who am I to deny the lady what she likes?” He sat next to me, handed me a plate, and then grabbed one for himself.

He picked up his phone and turned the music on quietly in the background while we enjoyed our meals. Once we finished, he stood up and brought everything inside. I got cozy and lay across the big bench covered in blankets and pillows. He returned with the coffee, and we sat and talked for hours.

I learned so much about him in those hours we spent underneath the stars. His mom and dad, Tamara and William, are still together, and he has three sisters: Clara, ten, and Rosie, who's 5.

His sister, Lynn, who is similar in age, is his adopted sister. Her parents were best friends with her parents, and they passed away in a tragic accident when she was only two years old, so Tamara and William adopted her.

He said he had a good childhood, and his parents may still be together, but he said he doesn't think they're in love. His dad was a real estate agent but travelled a lot for business, and his mom was a preschool teacher. He told me his passion was cooking and his pipe dream was to open his restaurant one day. When he told me his full name was Carter James Finley, he asked me what mine was.

"Olive Veronica Chambers"

"Do you have any siblings?"

"Just one brother, Sonny, and he's six years old. Product of my mom and stepdad, Richard. He adopted me when I was a baby because my biological father didn't want a kid, and thankfully, Richard took me in as his own. Sonny was an 'oops baby,' but it's been nice having him around. He keeps us all on our toes."

"Do you think about your biological dad? I'm sorry, but I am happy Richard was there for you, Olive. I hope I can meet them someday." Carter said, leaning into me.

"His name is Kenneth, and he's from Vancouver. Mom wanted to be home in Toronto. He was too preoccupied with his work to care about me, not enough anyway. He was a marine biologist, where my love for all things wildlife comes from. He passed away when I was about twelve years old. But it's okay." I said

"What's your goal in life?" He scooted closer to me, and then I rested my head on his lap, and he started to play with my hair.

"I mean, define a goal? I want to be a marine biologist. I start Uni in September in Vancouver. It's a biology course that allows me to get into my desired field. It's boring stuff. Are you going to go to school?" He looked down at me and started to graze his thumb across my cheekbone and down to my lips.

"Holy fuck." He said. "You are so fucking beautiful." I sat up, and he pulled me into his lap, but I turned and straddled him.

"I like you," I said, kissing him.

"What do you like about me?" He asked. I kissed him again.

"Hmm, your lips." We kissed again.

"Your eyes." I kissed the side of his lips.

"I like your kindness." I kissed his cheekbone.

"I like the way you look at me." I kissed his neck.

"I like the way I feel when we're together." I lingered there momentarily because the soft moans coming out of his mouth were enough to satisfy me. He slowly pulled away and cuffed his hands on my cheeks.

"Is this okay?" He looked deep into my eyes, and I had never been more sure that I wanted to be with him in every single way possible. I felt this energy whenever he was close to me; it was not something I wanted to lose. Even if I had to leave at the end of the summer, I knew he was concerned because of my assault, but the truth is, I didn't want that one thing to define who I was. I didn't want to lay awake at night and think that the last man who touched me was the one who violated me when I was drunk. I needed it as much as I wanted it.

"It's okay. I promise, Carter." I leaned in and let my lips graze his, my tongue entered his mouth, and we moved together in sync. He stood up, and I latched my legs around his waist and my arms around his neck.

'He leaned down slightly and popped the bench into a bed with one hand. He lowered me down and leaned over the top of me. The weight of his body made me warm, and the bulge in his jeans made me horny. It was dark, and we lay there kissing intently for a long time. The boat slowly rocked with each tiny wave that pushed through the water.

"I want to show you something." He rolled over to my side, gave me a clear sky view, and pointed up.

"Wow." I was stunned. I didn't think I had ever seen that many stars. I was born and raised in Toronto, and we didn't see as much there with all the lights from the city.

"Just wait." He propped himself up with one elbow, leaned over, and grabbed a switch. "Ready?" I nodded my head and smiled. He turned the lights off from the boat, and then we were in complete darkness, and the entire sky was lit with stars. We sat there in awe as I cuddled up to him.

"Thank you," I said.

"For what? You don't have to thank me. I like to make you smile."

"For everything."

I tilted my head and grabbed his face as our lips reached together. Our kisses were more fierce that time; you could tell the desire we felt for each other and how badly we both wanted this moment to happen. I brought my leg up slowly and pulled myself onto him. I tugged at his hair lightly.

"Fuck." He moaned in my ear. His hand moved down my chest and underneath my bra until his fingers reached my nipple, and he pinched it softly. I couldn't help the sounds coming out of my mouth.

"You like that?" he Whispers into my ear. I nodded my head and bit down on my lower lip. He smirked and took his hand out from under my bra.

"Take your clothes off," I demanded. Within seconds his clothes were tossed to the floor. We stayed there kneeling, facing each other when I put my arms up, and he slowly pulled my shirt over my head. I unbuttoned my jeans and slid them down my legs. I leaned back on the bench and used my elbows to prop myself up. I looked deep into his eyes and bit my lip. Hoping it was attractive and not creepy. I opened my legs, and he fell to his knees. He started kissing my inner knee, slowly reaching to my underwear. He grabbed the string of my thong, pulled it down and tossed it on the floor.

"I can't fucking wait to taste you." He lowered himself to my sex and took a lick like he had a lollipop in front of him. "So fucking good." I looked up into the sky and saw nothing but a sky full of stars, which was ironic because if I hadn't been literally underneath a sky full of stars, I would've thought I was having a case of Photopsia.

"Carter!" I screamed out his name. "Don't stop." I brushed my fingers through his hair, tugging it gently and held on tight as I slowly rocked against his face until I reached my climax. He slid up until we were face to face, and I grabbed his arms and forced him to his back before I started to crawl down him.

"No." He grabbed me and pulled me close to him. "I'm already hard for you, baby." I sat beside him, and his hard cock rested behind my ass. I started to kiss him from his lips, leading down to his chest.

"Condom?" I asked. He pulled his jeans up off the floor, reached into his wallet and pulled one out. I raised an eyebrow and smirked. He stopped and looked at me like he was worried about what I was about to say, and instead, I grabbed the condom from his hand, tore it open with my teeth, and slid it on him. I got on top of him, slowly eased myself onto him, and started to ride him as he moaned out my name.

"Olive, holy fuck, you are perfect." He pulled me close and whispered in my ear. "You are perfect, baby." His hands moved around my body, and he knew what to do to make me feel good.

We lay in each other's arms for hours, looking up into the sky. We laughed and pointed out shapes we could make out in the stars. Until we realized it was almost midnight, and the bugs started swarming. That was my favourite night we spent together. I knew he had stolen my whole heart.'

"You're doing it again, Dear! Are you still with me?" Agnus giggles.

"Fuck, I'm sorry," I replied.

"What's going on?" she shuffled closer to me.

"Sorry, my mind keeps wandering to our more 'sensual moments,' forgive me. It's been a while." I spit out.

"No, it's quite alright. I get what you mean. Can I ask you something?"

"Of course." I hope I didn't accidentally blurt something explicit and embarrass this poor old lady.

"How did you know you were ready to move on and be with someone else intimately after the awful thing that had happened to you? Did you feel pressured?" She seems concerned.

"Oh, god, no, it wasn't like that. I think that I just dealt with the trauma in a different way than the way you'd expect. I knew he had my heart that night, and I was ready for it. I had never shied away from sex before, but being with him was much more than that. He never pressured me or anything like that, ever." I reassure Agnus with the look in my eyes and the tone in my voice that I'm being truthful.

"So what's happened? Something must've happened between you two for you to be here in such a sad state. How long has it been now, since then, a year?"

"Yes, it's been about a year now." It has been, I know, because I've counted each day since we have been apart since I last tasted his lips and felt his arms around me. "Last month would've been exactly a year since I last saw him. Hard to believe because it feels like it has been an eternity. I pause and rub my hands on the bridge of my nose because I know I'm getting closer to the parts I'm not particularly eager to talk about.

The breeze outside starts to pick up, and I can feel it running through my hair and the howling of it brushing against the trees. A shiver crawls up my spine, and I think of the disappointment on Carter's face when I didn't show up at our meeting spot back in Elora. How could I be so heartless? I didn't reply to the letter out of pure bitterness that he hadn't contacted me sooner. But my very being is drawn to him, and my anxiety got the best of me.

"We can take a break if you'd like, Dear. Or continue another time if it's too hard for you?" Agnus can tell I am feeling a little uneasy, but I must finish the story, regardless of my reservations. Jay and Mila know my story. They know parts anyway, but truthfully - it's been too painful to recite from beginning to end. So this would be a first.

"Thanks, Agnus, but I'm okay. I can keep going." I said

♦ ♦ ♦

Chapter 8: The Tea Party

It made sense for Carter and me to spend most of our free time at his house, so we agreed when his parents asked if we could all have a nice sit-down dinner. We spent the nights at the motel so that we could have privacy, but the livelihood of his family's home sucked us back every time.

His little sisters had become one of the favourite parts of my days. They were a little devilish but such sweet, gentle souls. And the smiles they threw your way changed your mood instantly.

They had an idea. They wanted to have a family tea party. This point was when I had seen glimpses of his parents, and I had met his sisters here and there when Carter would babysit or take them for ice cream, but we had never had a sit-down '*this is my girlfriend*' introduction. His Mom wanted to meet me and see the girl who had stolen her only son's heart.

I wanted to make things perfect that day; my heart was all in. I got up early, went to the local dollar store, found fairy tiaras and wands, and picked them up. I went to the flower market and got flowers for Carter's Mom, and honestly, I didn't get anything for his dad. What do you get for a dad? Making their wives happy is good enough.

I showed up early and tried to see if I could do anything to help Tammy. When I called her Mrs. Finley, she told me it was silly to call her anything other than what her friends called her, and that was Tammy.

I placed scones onto platters and cupcakes onto the other ones, and we had soup, crackers, and little cut-out sandwiches. Tammy went all out for Clara and Rosie. I admired that a lot about her. She's a great mother. After we had everything prepared, I handed her the bouquet, and that's when she leaned into me and gave me a firm hug.

"Thank you, Olive." She walked toward her sink and pulled out a vase from underneath the cupboard. "You know, Carter's never brought any girls home before. For a while, we were concerned he felt nothing at all. When he told us about you, I thought *she must be something special*. I see that now. You're exceptional, Olive. I'm so happy you're here."

Well, where are the onions? Because that moment had me tearing up, it had her tearing up. Carter's intrusion, "Mom saved it. Are you making my girl cry?" He walked up to me, hugged me from behind, and kissed my back. He then walked up to his Mom and gave her a big hug.

"Oh, Stop it! You'll ruin my hair." She scuffed and then laughed.

"You'll ruin my hair." Carter mimicked his Mom and then walked away, but not before she threw Brussels sprouts at the back of his head and stuck her tongue out at him. I just sat and laughed with

her. I could enjoy moments like this because I missed being back home.

Outside was a dream. Tammy had a real knack for decor and hosting. White lace canopies were hanging from the trees to the far left. Wooden skids on the ground with white lace tablecloths overtop. Each of us had our placemat with our names and a teacup.

Clara had me sit next to her and Carter on my other side. I pulled out the two little gift bags and handed one to Clara and the other to Rosie, who squealed, grabbed the bag and started tearing it apart. Clara carefully pulled the tissue paper out, unfolded everything neatly, and said, "Thank you, Miss Olive." And bowed her head - she was committed to her tea party. Conversations went smoothly throughout the day, which impressed both Carter and me.

Carter assumed that his dad would fuck up conversations and make things awkward; I guess he was known for that kind of thing. Meanwhile, I thought I would be the one to make things weird. I walked off on my own toward the path leading to their pond. I needed to stretch my legs.

When I got closer, I saw Clara hunched over. Her body moved and whimpered like she was sobbing. So I approached her and asked her what was wrong. She confided in me that she had a crush on a girl in her class who was a bully and made fun of her in front of their friends.

I told her that, in four years, none of this would matter. Keeping her head up and heartbreak is part of life. I told her not to let them bring her down or dim her shine because she was a wonderful human being and that one day she would meet someone who won't even have a thought in their mind about hurting her, and that she was still so very young and that sometimes people can be cruel but that it was essential to stick up for ourselves without being cruel in return.

"So, what do I do when I feel like I'm just about to go crazy from anger and embarrassment?" She wiggles her nose in disgust and stiffens her shoulders. That makes me smile.

"Can I tell you a story, kiddo?" I kneel on the grass next to her.

"Okay…"

"I was nine years old. There was this awful student in my class named Rodney Bush. He would tease me whenever he could. I always ignored it, as my Mom told me to. One day, my anger built up so badly. I walked to the front of the class to present my project. I worked hard on it, and I was excited to show it. He ran up to me as I approached the front, poked me in the belly, and oinked. Outraged as I possibly could, I grabbed my teacher's coffee mug and tossed it at him. He stepped backward, dodging it but tripped and broke his arm when he landed on it."

"Right on!" Clara cheers for me. "He deserved it."

"That's not my point, Clara. I ruined everyone's day, including my own. I was suspended for a week and grounded for months. My parents were so disappointed in me. Did he deserve it? Maybe he did. But it wasn't worth it in the end. If I had just ignored it and moved on, I would have saved myself so much time of sadness and loneliness." I nudged her arm.

"Do you see what I mean?" She smiles, but I can tell she's holding back. If she doesn't fully trust, that's how it will be for her.

"You know that whatever she said wasn't true. Often bullies say mean things to you because they're trying to keep the attention off of themselves."

"Clara, time to get ready for bed! You have an early day tomorrow." Tammy yells from the stairs. So we get up and start walking back to the house.

"Thank you, Olive." She smiles and waves and retreats inside the house.

Later on, back at the motel. Carter and I lay in bed, watching TV and eating snacks until we were so full we couldn't move. "Thanks for coming today," Carter said to me.

"My family seems to love you, Ol." He sits up on the bed and faces me.

"I like them too. Your sisters are adorable. Clara is so smart. I would love to spend more time with them too. If that would be okay?" I insisted. Carter pushed all the wrappers off the bed and looked at me like an animal.

"What the fuck?" I laughed. "What are you doing?"

He gets to his knees and grabs me, pulling me onto his lap. He leans close to my face, the heat between us building quickly. His lips inches from mine, he leans in until we're touching, and then he nibbles on my lip and pulls back.

"Have I ever told you how fucking perfect you are?." He lowered me to the bed and slid his hands down my body, stopping at the rim of my pants and pulling them off swiftly. I moan into his ear with each movement he takes...."

Present

"Olive!! My Jesus." Agnus looks petrified, her cheeks went red, but she laughed and slapped my knee playfully.

"My bad, Agnus." Shit. I keep forgetting she's even here. Sometimes for a second, I'm dreaming the whole thing out again.

"You get the idea. Things got spicy."

♦ ♦ ♦

Chapter 9 The Summer

Past

I spent most of my days at the aquarium, doing anything Ronnie needed from me. I would clean out the tanks, feed the fish, and ensure things were up to date and organized and the water stayed in tip-top shape for all the fish or wildlife he had. Occasionally, I'd see Nancy working simultaneously as me, and she would converse with me, but I kept it short. My goal was and always has been to do anything involved with saving wildlife, so this was a start. Anything that paid and got me away from home was a bonus.

The days Carter was there helping out at Elora Reef, we would flirt from across the room. He would walk by and grab my ass when nobody was looking or pull me into the changing rooms in the back for a make-out session. I took it any second I could get alone with him, even to stare into his eyes. After work, we would fall into each other's arms and the sheets. We did it anywhere and everywhere possible. Carter had picked me up from work once, and he was driving this time, which we don't often do because it makes the most sense to walk, but we expected a storm. We parked at the side of the road and had sex in the back seat, having to dodge the cars driving by so they couldn't see us there. It was the most exhilarating moment for me. I had never done anything that crazy before.

We fit together. Everything about us felt right. We would try to do things together on the weekends, like; spending our days under the sun at the beach, he taught me how to fish, and we even went camping for one night until he realized it wasn't my thing. Regardless, we were inseparable.

I spent much time over at his parent's house, babysitting his little sisters, whom I had adored. Clara was ten, and she reminded me of a mini Carter. She's intelligent, funny, and charming. She has bright big green eyes, just like Carter does too. Whenever she caught us going for a kiss, she would yell, "Ewwwwwww." Rosie was five and the sweetest thing, always smiling and laughing. She had blonde hair with thick curly locks, half taken from his father's side and a half from his Mom's. His Mom had dark hair like Carter, but it was curly. You could tell it used to have more to it, but over time it fell into more of a wave. And then there was his sister Lynne, aka the friend of my nemesis. Why would I befriend such a horrible human being if we can even call her that? Katrina the destroyer, more like it. Half human, half demon. Despite all this,

Lynn and I became semi-friends while I was at her home, getting to know everyone. She still hangout with Katrina, but for the most part, she kept her at a distance when we were around. She was a good person, just led by shitty people. She'd find her way, but I grew to like her.

Although we spent every free moment together - I was never sure how I felt about his dad, and I think he felt the same about me. I never did anything wrong, but he has a strong work ethic, and he assumed I'd hold him back. I never cared to try to impress him, as that's just who I've always been, plus he seemed like a bit of an asshat. His Mom was one of the sweetest women I had ever met, she adored me, and I adored her. She felt like coming home, like all the happiness and kindness in the world. It somehow lived in her.

It would sometimes sadden me when she made me feel like family, knowing I would be leaving come summer's end. And I just knew I didn't want to leave. I wasn't ready. Who wants to go to a place that feels like home? I belong here more than I do back home.

On the days we didn't spend together, I felt empty and bored - even though most of the time, we just existed together. I would work, and watch TV, and he would take day trips to visit his Grams, and that made me happy that he loved her so much.

There was this particular date that I adored, of ours and it was mid-summer. We had only been together for a short time, but it felt like a lifetime. Being with Carter was like living in some fantasy magical realm that runs differently in time. How is it that nearly a month of knowing him feels like years? I refuse to think of the moment we'll have to part. He will meet someone new somehow, and *Poof*, I'm forgotten. It's not like I'm all that memorable. I'm a basic, ordinary woman. I put little effort into my day-to-day looks. More times than not, I toss my hair in space buns or a messy one on the top of my head. Over the years of dying and curling/straightening my hair, my natural beachy waves turned into ratty crimps. I don't have the time to do anything else with it. My favourite outfits usually include overalls or cropped tops - I still wear those.

Anyway, my point is this - if I'm ordinary and 'basic,' who am I to say that Carter won't find someone much more appealing in every way possible? I've always been the one who puts the most effort into relationships and never had the same in return. My ex-boyfriend, Tanner, told me one time during a fight and then again at the end,

'Olive, look at you. You're basic. You should have just accepted this for what it was. You were *lucky* to be with me. You were *lucky* that I was even here. I should have never been your boyfriend, and I'm over it.' I wouldn't call myself lucky. When I met Tanner, it was at a party my friends dragged me to; I had been out of a previous relationship for about four months. When I got to the party, he was there, Will. The first relationship I had, went down in atomic bombs.

He told everyone I cheated on him to spite me. And in return, I made him feel much worse. So back to the party, I had just arrived, and my ex, Will, wanted to talk, and next thing I knew, he was trying to stick his tongue down my throat and grope my ass. I didn't have it, so I pulled away and explained that I wasn't going back down this road, to which he said, "Who else is going to fuck you? Nobody." I walked away to the nearest attractive guy I could find. I said,

"My ex is insulting and trying to get with me, and I'm pretty uncomfortable - He says nobody else will 'fuck' me, and I want him to back off. Can we hang out?" The blue-eyed guy who would soon try to ruin me; smirked, pulled his hand out to shake mine and said,

"I'm Tanner." he looked up, and about ten feet away from us were Will and his brother staring in our direction. He smirked at them and then put his arm around my shoulder. "Want a drink?"

And that night, I got extraordinarily drunk and fell asleep in a park. Tanner sat next to me and waited until I woke so that I would be safe. Ironic, right? Because shortly after that, well, the rest is history and not a great one, either. Nonetheless, I've had many bad experiences with men, so you can't blame me for how I am.

♦ ♦ ♦

Chapter 10: The Family Reunion

Our sweet summer bliss ended the night of the bonfire.

It was the end-of-season bonfire where the town gathered to burn 'old memories.' Something you wanted to forget, whether it was old furniture, diaries, photos, or memories of people. It was a chance to get together and burn your trash. It was odd, but I loved participating in their weird town traditions.

I was also excited because Mila was coming with her boyfriend Wyatt for the weekend, and I hadn't seen her since I left for the summer.

Mila has been my best friend/sister since I was a baby. Her dad was best friends with my stepfather. Her dad had passed away in a tragic hit-and-run accident when she was fifteen, and she never fully recovered from it. Her Mom had been at home with Mila and not at work, where she was a doctor. She always said she wondered if she could've tried to help save him or be with him in his last moments. But her Mom had been home with a cold, *'a freakin cold.'* She always said. Something switched in her Mom that day, and she was never the same. Her Mom wasn't the most incredible mother to Mila after

that, often leaving her alone or without meals prepped and ready for her; she did everything alone. My Mom and Richard took her in, so she spent much time at our house.
It worked out for us because we were inseparable before we could walk. When we were 15, Mila met Wyatt, who has been part of our little clique since then. I don't have any complaints. I like him a lot, and I know they are soulmates. Sometimes I just needed girl time, and he was always there. Anyway, I was excited to see them. The night of the bonfire had also been the day Carter's family had a massive get-together at their home in the backyard, where they had tents set up for dining and dancing. They did it every year with friends and family. There was never a specific reason; it was just a celebration for the end of the summer and a reason to get everyone together.

Over the last month, Carter began sleeping with me at the motel every night. We didn't like spending too much time with his parents because we didn't have the privacy we wanted. I knew today would be a big day for everyone, so I got up early and ran to Franny's to get Carter and my coffee and muffins for breakfast.

There was something in the pit of my stomach telling me something would go wrong today. I remember having this feeling twice throughout my life, and the thoughts made me feel so ill. I tried to push it away both previous times, and low and behold — shit always went wrong, no matter what. So I knew it would happen this time, too.

The first time I was in fifth grade, I told my Mom that I was sick, and she refused to let me stay home because she said I looked physically fine and had no temperature. She made me go to school, even when I pleaded not to. Everything was normal when I got to my classroom and sat down. Our principal walked in, teary-eyed and nervous. That's when he told us that one of the girls, two grades higher, had taken her life by suicide and that if anyone needed counselling, it was available. Just like that, the entire school had turned to chaos. I stood up and ran for the bathroom but didn't make it. I puked all over the classroom door, and the crying students exited the room, giving me saddened glances as they passed by me. It was a nightmare, and I didn't leave my room until my Mom forced me out a week later.

The second time wasn't until grade ten. I recognized the feeling as soon as I opened my eyes that day. I had thought about skipping out of school and hiding all day, but I pushed the thoughts away, telling myself that whatever it was - I could handle it. Walking into my school was a fucking nightmare. People were staring more than usual, laughing and whispering with their friends, looking down at their phones and then back at me. I sent my first nude at 16 to the exchange student, Fabio. He told me I was hot and that he was only thinking of me, so naturally, I sent him a nude. He must have shown some douchebag at my school because the photo spread to everyone. Why don't I listen to my gut when telling me something is wrong? I had zero ideas.

I pushed the thoughts away, dismissing them as anxiety because my best friend was coming to visit me and meet Carter. I told myself to relax and enjoy the day, but the feeling wouldn't disappear.

Back at home, when I'd have anxieties, I would go for walks and clear my head; *but back at home*, I know the in's and out's, I know how to stay hidden when I don't want to be alone, and here, I can't do that yet.

I hear a knock at the door, and when I pull it open, I see Mila and Wyatt standing before me. I squeal and jump at her, giving her the tightest hug possible. It takes a moment to realize that Jay is standing behind them. So I push through Mila and Wyatt to get to Jay. "Had to come to see my girl." He flashes a devilish grin. So I playfully nudge him, and I walk back inside.

"Hey, Wyatt." I stop and laugh. "Just kidding!" I pull him in for a brotherly hug. Mila looks toward me and rolls her eyes with a playful scuff.

"I missed you, Ollie. Where's the lover boy?" She looks around the room. "We're staying in the room next door to you. I already dropped everything off before I came here." She adds.

"Well, hello, everyone." Carter walks out of the bathroom, smelling like freshly showered goodness, probably one of my favourite scents. I suddenly start to imagine us when we shower together. I swear I could live in that scent. Whatever he uses there, it's magic to my nostrils. He greets everyone in the room before stopping next to me and putting his arm around my waist. "How was the ride?" He asks.

"Not bad." Mila and Wyatt reply in unison.

"Was fucking horrid. Mila made me listen to teeny bop bullshit the whole way here!" Jay shouts. Mila mimics him and scowls his way.

"Anyway, what's the plan? Mila said some bonfire was happening tonight?" Jay asks,

"It's an annual thing. It gives people a reason to trash things they don't want and drink. It's a good time." Carter says. "My family has a big dinner slash after party in our backyards with tents and a band, and you're all welcome to come." He adds.

"Awesome, let's get ready!" Mila shouts; she grabs my arm and pulls me toward the door.

"Already? It doesn't start for like… 8 hours." Carter seems confused.

"Yes, exactly, we're on the clock!" She shouts.

5 o'clock comes fast. I'm impressed with how Mila made me look. Mila always makes me look stunning, with my hair curled and half tucked back. She brought the lacey black long-sleeve shirt that she knows I'm obsessed with paired with a black undershirt. I wore my high-waisted black jeans and small heel boots. I had an oversized pink jacket that I threw over top. Mila did my makeup elegantly, and I'm curious to know how she always does it. My efforts are maximum with little success.

We agreed to dinner at Carter's parents, so we headed for his house first. I texted to let him know we were on our way, but when I picked up my phone, I noticed he had already texted me.

Carter:

See you soon, baby

I swear - I get weak when he calls me that. I've always hated pet names. My ex-boyfriend used to call me "sweetie," and it creeped me out. Felt like he was my grandpa or something. I knew this couple in high school who would always make out in the hallways, everyone knew them for that, and they'd always call each other baby, and it would make me cringe. With Carter, it was different. It made me want to strip his clothes off and attack him with my lips.

I push away all my sexual thoughts and head for the door. We all walk out, and I lead the way. Mila and Wyatt walk behind Jay and me. Carter's house is about 10-15 minutes from the motel. "So, how are things?" I look toward Jay.

"Oh, you know, the usual" we continue walking, but Jay slows down, letting Mila and Wyatt walk in front of us.

"Just keep walking straight; I'll tell you when to turn," I shout. Jay and I always end up in the back because Mila doesn't like the smell of the smoke, and it always blows in her face. Jay sparks up a joint and takes a pull. "Any news with the guy?" Jay's energy shifts. He seems uncomfortable.

"Uh, honestly? It's not great. I mean, he's not ready to come out; he has a girlfriend and is embarrassed to be who he is. Why would I want that?" He hands the joint to me, and I gladly take it, taking a few puffs and thinking about my response.

"Do you love him?"

"I mean, love is a strong word. I feel differently for him than before and stupidly stick around. Hoping he will change."

"Are you going to tell me who it is, Jay?" I cough and hand back the joint to him.

"It's not important enough to tell you yet. I promise I will when the time is right." When I look up, we are approaching the Finley house. I'll never get over how extravagant it is.

The grass is greener than ever on this side, quite literally. There is a big willow tree that hangs over part of the front of the home. It is two floors, a deck wrapping around the entire house on both levels, and it's completely white with black shutters on each window. There's a beautiful giant staircase leading to wooden white double doors. They had plants to add some colour and flower pots hanging around. I stand there for a second to catch my breath before I lift my hand to knock, but before I first reach the door, it swings open, and I sway forward, almost losing my balance. I stand straight and pull my coat down to adjust myself. That was a close one.

"Fuck, you look stunning," Carter licks his lips and pulls me in for a hug. He kisses the side of my head and whispers in my ear, "can't fucking wait to rip this dress off you later." I shyly giggle and walk

into the house, and Mila, Wyatt and Jay enter behind.
When we get to the backyard, they've got tents outside. There was one for dining and one for dancing. There are so many people, and it's overwhelming. Carter walks us toward the far end, where his immediate family sits. I recognize his closest friends, Gabe and Ace. Gabe shifted in his seat and whispered something into Katrina's ear, and they laughed. I wasn't too fond of the vibe I was getting. I hated her, and as far as I knew, I didn't like Gabe either. He was shifty. Ace smiled and waved. He has copper-coloured hair with little curls throughout it and freckles that fill his nose and spread out toward his cheeks. Something about him screamed good energy. Carter's dad sat at the end of the table, and his Mom sat on the opposite side. Carter sat directly across from his Mom and beside his dad, and I sat beside him. Jay was beside me, and then Wyatt and Mila.

"Cheers to Ma, who can't make it today because she has a sore throat and is cuddled up in bed." Carter's dad shouted and raised his glass,

"To Grams!" Carter said, "We love you!"

The next few hours went by quickly, and everything was going well, other than a few uncomfortable looks from Gabe and Katrina. Jay seemed off, his eyes wouldn't stop wandering, and I swear I saw Gabe glance at him. He seemed sad - it only lasted seconds before he wiped the frown off his face and started to fake a smile. When I looked toward the water, I realized how close his house was to the lake. The sun is setting fast, and things get uncomfortable when his dad has had one too many and can't stop blabbing his mouth.

"So, son, are you all ready to leave at the end of the month? My boy! So proud you decided to take my advice for once and join the army. Very noble." I pause. He pauses, and instant panic reaches his eyes. He looks at me and back toward his dad. I wait for his answer.

"Uhh… yeah." He can't seem to form his words which are when my heart and stomach both drop simultaneously. *Where the fuck is he going. He's never once mentioned going anywhere. Now I'm mad. I want to know what the fuck is going on.* So I yelled. Loud.

"What the fuck, Carter?" Everyone went quiet and stared at me as I stood up and pushed my hair back out of my face. "Where are you going? Please, why don't you explain to me." He quickly got to his feet and tried to grab my arms to pull me to the side lightly. He didn't say a word. So I looked toward his dad.

"Please, Mr. Finley, fill me in because your son is lost for his words." I cross my arms in a '*don't fuck with me'* stance. He has no problem yelling out his son's secret when he realizes he has been lying to me this entire time. The corner of his mouth raises a half smile before he says it,

"Well, dear, he's going to the Army.. Didn't he tell you? Oh, boy…." he huffed loudly and glared at his son. "Well, go on, everyone - nothing to see." The voices continued as if nothing had even happened. "Jesus, son, you sure like to make a scene." He huffed again, but I could tell by his stance that he was relaxed - part of him liked to embarrass Carter, which hurt my heart, even with the anger burning inside me.

"Thanks for dinner, it was lovely, but I'll be going now." I looked at his parents with the fakest smile I could ever give. I didn't care that my purse and jacket were inside; I needed to escape. I couldn't breathe. I started to walk away, and when Carter tried to yell my name and follow behind me, I stopped hastily and turned around. "Don't fucking follow me. I need space," and then I storm off.

It only took me minutes to reach the harbour, and it was already filled with people drinking and families huddled up under blankets, all waiting for the bonfire to start. I went down the path where it was quieter, and I started thinking hard. Carter had been lying to me. He was going to the Army and didn't want to tell me. He couldn't be honest with me about something so important, which means he could've lied about other things too. My chest physically hurt, and I realized why I had been off all day. My stomach hadn't once led me on. I should've known.

As I strolled down the path, my arms crossed because I was cold. I noticed a shadow of a person leaning against a tree, and my stomach dropped; I heard the crunching of sticks as he walked off the grass and toward me. It was him—the assaultant. I couldn't move. I couldn't think. Why the fuck was he there?

"Hi." His voice was more profound than I remembered, and my heart was racing so fast I might have had a heart attack. It was fight or flight. He took a step toward me, and I backed up.

"Stay the fuck back," I shouted. "What do you want? Why are you here? You've taken enough from me." I held back the tears so hard I felt like I might've exploded.

"I'm sorry. I was drunk. You have to know that's not who I am. I can't stop thinking about you." He stepped forward again, smiling, he had no remorse, and I could tell by the look in his eyes that he was deranged, probably drunk or high.

"I don't give a fuck." I pulled my arm up and swung it so fast until it collided with his nose. Fuck. That hurt. He stumbled back and then held onto his nose.

"You fucking bitch." He walked toward me, but Carter came running toward him and tackled him before he could get close. He started swinging, but this guy ran his mouth with each punch.

"You stupid slut." Punch.

"You deserved it." Double punch.

I started to get worried when Carter didn't stop swinging, and I finally returned to reality; I started screaming at him to stop.

"He's not fucking worth it." I grabbed Carter's arm, and he stopped right away. He looked down at the bloodied face, back up at me, and stood up. Before we walked away, I turned him over, grabbed his wallet, opened it, and found his ID. Blake Trenton. I took a photo of it, tossed it on the floor beside him, and walked away, pulling Carter with me.

Once we had been far from Blake, I stopped dead in my tracks and looked at Carter. "Are you okay?" He asked me; *I'm not okay, but I'm here*, I think to myself. All the anger and sadness I had felt toward him had left as quickly as they came, I grabbed him as soon as I possibly could and wrapped my arms around his waist and rested my head on the crease of his neck, and I just sobbed. He didn't say anything. He let me cry and rubbed my back until the whimpers broke. I could hear his heart beating beyond the sounds of people partying and laughing all around us.

"I'm sorry." He sighed.

"Not right now, please. Can we go enjoy the bonfire?" I pleaded,

"Okay." I looked up at his beautiful aqua-coloured eyes, which in the dark looked greener, and I cupped his face with my hand. I leaned in for a gentle kiss and then grabbed his hand in mine, and we walked toward the bonfire, keeping our eyes peeled for Mila and Wyatt.

Present

Agnus shrieks and then wipes the tears that have slid down her face. "I'm so sorry, Dear. You poor thing, you have been through so much, haven't you?"

"It's okay, Agnus. Thank you." I've had enough time to accept what happened to me entirely, and although it's horrible, it led to many great things in my life. Blake Trenton will forever haunt me, but it doesn't define who I am. I'm none of those things he described me to be. He's an awful person, and I honestly could never see him again, and it would be too soon for me. "That's not even where the night ended. Are you ready for the rest of it?" She nods and smiles.

♦ ♦ ♦

Chapter 11 The Bonfire

Carter and I finally made our way toward the bonfire when we spotted Mila and Wyatt, who seemed slightly out of place in the Dance Tent. So I rushed to their side, apologized, and asked where Jay was. She said he ran off to smoke, so I pulled my phone out and texted him.

Meet by the bonfire.

He hadn't responded, so we left the tent and headed toward the bonfire. Mila slipped me some rum in a flask tucked safely in her purse. I could tell she was drinking because she's way more extroverted when drunk. When we walked up, Carter noticed Gabe in the corner of his eye, and he walked toward him.

"Wait." I grabbed his arm. "I'm going to look for Jay. I'll catch up, okay?" I reached up and kissed him on the lips.

"I'm coming! Go with Carter, okay, Sweetie? I love you!" Mila wrapped her arms so tight around Wyatt and kissed him at least twenty times before she smacked his ass and walked away.

"Watch her." He mouthed toward me before he walked off with Carter. Mila stumbled toward me and linked her arm to mine. We pushed through people to reach the big wooden boat you tossed your things in. I pulled out the clothes I wore my first night there, the day of the assault. I wanted to throw them away for a while, but something inside me kept putting them back in the bottom of the suitcase. I tossed them into the boat and turned toward Mila, who was pulling papers out of her purse; she looked down at them and said,

"Fuck you, Harvard," And threw the pile of papers into the boat.

When I glanced across the boat, I saw Jay peeking out from behind the pile of junk stacking up in the boat. He looked sad.

"Look," I nudged Mila's arm. We both walked toward him, and when we got closer, we noticed that he had a photograph in his hands. When he saw us approaching him, he took the photo and tossed it into the boat, but it landed in the sand, and Mila ran up to it and gasped. Jay tried to grab it, but it was too late.

"What the fuck, Jay?" She looked disappointed. "This guy?" She scuffed it and handed it to me. It took me a second to realize who it was.

"Seriously? You told me it wasn't anything to worry about, and I think being my boyfriend's best fucking friend would mean something to you. And he's gay? What about Katrina?" Jay stood there, stunned.

“What about Katrina?” She came out of nowhere, guards up because she heard us saying her name. My mind started to race, we had no time to control the situation. “Oh la la, what’s that you got?” Katrina drunkenly snatched the photo out of my hand and waved it around. Jay's face went completely pale and he just stood there silently. I jumped at her, trying to take the photo back from her hands.

"It's none of your business, give it back!" I demanded. She didn't listen, and my stomach dropped.

"Are you fucking kidding me? This is why he dumped me, for you?" She challenged.

"Fuck you!" Jay warned, taking a step forward. Katrina stepped forward and wiped a single tear off her cheek.

"You know what, he's not even worth it. He's a tool." She said, before tossing the photo on the ground and walking off.

"Can I explain?" He led us to a quiet spot on the beach, and we sat down; he told us that he met Gabe the night he came into town, and they made out, but he was 'straight' and drunk, which was a mistake. It wasn't until the night of the carnival that they hooked up when everyone was distracted, and then Gabe freaked out afterwards, ashamed of who he was and stormed off. Jay said that Gabe reached out, and they would meet secretly from Toronto to Elora, even when he was at home. Things got too severe for him, and Katrina got suspicious, and he pulled away, so Jay showed up, leading up to the bonfire.

"I love him. I know I'm fucking stupid. But I do." He pouted. He put his knees up to his head and crunched over, and I could tell he was crying. Jay doesn't cry, so when I saw it, my heart broke, and my devil horns came out because what I did next was ruthless. Maybe the rum and coke also had something to do with it, but I didn't care.

"Fuck this!" I shouted and grabbed the photo from Jay and stood up and pushed through people, looking for this fucker. Jay and Mila follow behind me, trying to tell me it's a bad idea and not to go there. I went there. I saw Carter and Gabe standing alon, and screamed as I got closer.

"You piece of shit!" It took Carter a moment to realize I wasn't talking to him when I stormed past him and aimed for Gabe's face with my fist. Then I started punching his chest before Carter pulled me off of him and placed me on the ground,

"Olive, what's going on?" He genuinely looks confused.

"Why don't you tell him, GAY-be?" I darted my eyes toward him. Jay and Mila finally catch up, and Jay looks at Gabe with a sadness I've never seen in him before.

"I'm sorry." He said to him,

"Did you just punch my boyfriend?" Katrina walked up behind us with her posse following behind.

"That's fucking just great. Just what we needed." I mumble under my breath.

"Excuse me? What the fuck is going on, Gabe?" He didn't say a word. He just stood there hoping she'd stop talking, but she didn't. She walked right up to him and grabbed his arm possessively.

"Let's get out of here." She demanded.

"No."

"What?" She looked surprised and pissed off, maybe a bit embarrassed too.

"I'm not going anywhere with you; we are done," Gabe shouted, releasing his arm from her grip.

"Are you fucking kidding me?" She slapped him hard and walked off. Good for her, I mean, she was horrible, but her boyfriend was secretly gay and screwing my best friend, so there's that. Everyone stood still for a minute, stunned, taking in what had just happened. Jay looked up at us and stormed off; Gabe followed him immediately without hesitation.

"Woohoo, what's happening?" Mila slurred.

"This is our queue. I'm bringing Mila back to the motel." Wyatt picked up Mila and started to walk off with her, but I shouted,

"Bonfire first? It might sober her up. PLEASE," I beg, facing Wyatt. I didn't want the night to end and missed my best friend dearly. We needed more time together.

"Please! I need to hang out with my bestie." I stomped on the ground and pouted like a toddler not getting their way.

"Ugh. Okay." Wyatt shifted Mila, now holding bridal style and walked her toward the bonfire. "Let's get you some fries." And he walked toward the fry stand, leaving Carter and me in silence. After a few moments pass.

"So Gabe is gay?" Carter started laughing hysterically. "I guess that answers some questions I've always had." I joined him and started laughing too. I had almost forgotten the drama we had between us for a second. Almost.

"Should I be worried for Jay?" I looked at Carter and leaned in for a hug, and I think he could tell by my expression; the sighs and wide eyes- I wasn't playing anymore. The jokes were over, and my genuine concern for Jay, one of my best friends, was apparent. I would be damned if I let some asshole mess with him. Whether he's Carter's best friend or not.

"No, Gabe is a good guy. I promise. I don't know what's going on with him, but despite that, he's a great dude."

When we found Mila and Wyatt, they had been cuddled together at the beach. Mila was still very drunk, and poor lovely Wyatt was sober as he could be.

Only a few minutes had passed before the bonfire had lit up in flames; ten minutes later, it was so high I swear it lit up the entire town. They were right, though. There was something incredibly soothing knowing that the outfit I tossed in there had been burned to a crisp in that bonfire. After things had died down, it got quiet, and we somehow managed to stay there all that time, just talking. Mila was falling asleep in Wyatt's arms, and I was sitting there snuggled up to Carter while he and Wyatt spoke about things they had in common; their love for cars, video games, and movies.

It was nice knowing that Carter got along with Wyatt because he was a massive part of my life since he was in love with my best friend.

"How did you and Mila meet?" Carter asked Wyatt. I laughed. Their meet-cute was a good story, and I zoned in on him as I cuddled Carter next to the fire.

"It was Junior year. I was nervous as hell about starting high school. I had friends, but many of my friends and I were separated in our classes since we couldn't pick our courses. I sat in the back right corner, unnoticed. There was this guy, Mark. He was a total asshat. He always teased people, but I didn't want to get on his wrong side, so I often just sat there and let it happen. Anyway, he had told me that Cindy, the blonde girl with big boobs, wanted to go out with me, and I *had to do it* because her friend was also going, and he wanted to be set up. You get the point.

So I went on this group date, and it was at a local diner I had never been to before since I was new in town, and it was an absolute disaster. Mark's date said he was an asshole and stormed off; somehow, that turned Cindy on, and they started making out in the booth in front of me. They got up and left a few minutes later, leaving me with the bill.

The waitress approached me and said, "That sucks. I'm sorry." then laughed. I was so embarrassed, but then she nudged me, looked into my eyes, and flat-out said,

"Listen, shit happens. She's a nitwit, and so is he. They are perfect for each other, and you're too good for her." She picked up the tab and said, "Don't worry about it." Smiling at me as she walked away. I knew right then and there that she was something special. I waited for her to finish her shift and then walked her home. We've been together ever since."

I sat before the man who loved my best friend and had never heard his version of their story. I turned my head and quickly wiped the tear on my cheek before anyone noticed.

"True romantic," Carter said, facing Wyatt.

"So when are you going to ask her to marry you?" I trawled, trying to get answers from him. But as he opened his mouth to speak, Mila nudged herself awake and lifted her head from his shoulder, groggy and still very intoxicated.

"Hi, babe." She smiled up at Wyatt and grabbed his face for a sloppy kiss. When she finished, Wyatt looked up at us, winked, and mouthed, "Soon." As the fire started to shrink slowly, so did our energy.

"We should head back." Wyatt stood to his feet and grabbed Mila bride and groom style, and they waved before he carried her back.

—

We had planned to sleep in the boat to give Jay his privacy. All my things were at Carter's parent's house, so we retreated that way. We tried to avoid the commotion of the after-hours party still going on with all of the stranglers hanging around. We slipped through the side door unnoticed. All the lights were off in the house to keep people from going there. So we tiptoed through the living room. I headed for the stairs to go to Carter's bedroom, got my bags, and then headed right for the door as quickly as possible.

"God, I'm so angry." Carter shouts, "I wanted to tell you myself" I kept walking past him, heading for the stairs.

"Whatever, you weren't going to tell me, Carter. Someone had to. Can we talk later? I need some air." I said

"I'll come with you."

"No." I looked back at him, as I was a few steps further down than he was and nodded, *'We're fine.'*

"I'm walking you home." Carter grabbed my arm gently and turned me toward him. His hands touching me makes my temperature rise, and my cheeks turn red. I was about to forget about it and kiss him when I reminded myself that I wouldn't deal with this drama.

"Olive, please stop." Carter stopped walking and sighed in defeat. I stopped, but I didn't turn around. I wait for his excuses. "I didn't tell you because I didn't want it to define our relationship. I'm going to the Army and doing training; I will be gone for six months to a year." I couldn't stand it anymore, so I turned around and yelled,

"So what the fuck, Carter? What was all this stuff about wanting to own a restaurant? You had many opportunities to open up and be honest with me, but you weren't. Instead, you lied. What else have you lied about? Do you even care about me, or was this all bullshit?"

"I am going to be a chef. A military chef." He said sarcastically. I tried to slow down and lower my voice, but as the words flew out of my mouth, I got even angrier and more upset. He fell his head into his hands, stood tall, and ran his fingers through his hair. He does this when he's feeling awkward and doesn't know what to say.

"I'm an idiot. I'm sorry. I didn't want to ruin what we started. And to be fair, I'm not lying; I do want to be a chef, and I do want to own a restaurant one day, but I have to do this first. I can't explain it, Ol, but I must do this. My grandfather Charles did this for his entire life. He fought for our country. I figured this was the best of both worlds: my passion and my grandpa's. So, I have to do this. I don't expect you to wait for me, but I want to spend the rest of my time with you if you let me." He stepped forward and grabbed my hands, and slid his fingers into mine. "I love you. There I said it. I love you, Olive." He stared at me, smiling, but there was sadness in his eyes.

"What? Carter, are you serious?"

"Yes, Ol, I love you. You are it for me. I don't care if it's only been a few months. It's been the best summer of my life. I've never felt like this before. I love you so much it hurts." I hesitated, but I knew that I loved him. I knew that he made me feel special and that I felt like nothing else mattered when we were together. I knew that when I bit my lower lip, it drove him insane. I knew he had a small spot under his ear that tickled when I kissed it; I knew that he pretended not to like my music and the movies I watched but that he secretly enjoyed them. I adored so many details and little things about him, and it all joined together, making me fall so deeply in love with him that it terrified me to the core.

"I love you too… but…." My chin started to quiver, and my heart started to race.

"You're leaving, and so am I. What does that mean for us?" I couldn't hold back tears any longer, my heart was utterly shattered at that moment, and I realized that when Carter left, he would take a piece of me with him. He pulled me into a long hug and let me cry into his chest. There was a reason I held off thinking of this moment until now.

After several horrible, snot-filled minutes, I pulled myself together, wiped my face with my sleeve and pushed my head into his chest, stretching back to give myself some space. I slid my hand behind his neck and kissed him softly, tasting my tears, unprepared for 'us' to end.

I felt like the 'see you laters' were all happening too fast. We woke in the morning and met Mila and Wyatt for brunch at the diner. Mila told us how she had a blast, but her head was pounding, and she couldn't wait to return to her bed.

Mila sat next to Wyatt across from Carter and me, and she leaned her head on Wyatt's arm for the majority of the time. I ordered a big meal, and so did Carter, we were up to nonsense last night, and I had an empty stomach with a full heart - which called for a lovely brunch.

"I'm going to be sick," Mila shouted, her face paler than her usual warm skin tone.

"Well, don't do it over here. I'm trying to eat!" I stuck my tongue out playfully,

"Do you need help, babe?" Wyatt turns toward her with concern in his eyes. She shook her head 'no.' and darted for the bathroom.

"I'll be back." I stood up promptly and headed for the bathroom, Mila hates throwing up, and it gives her anxiety the same way it does for me. When we were in sixth grade Mila got her period, which would give her such bad pain that she would be nauseous the entire time. We were in class, and I heard our secret tap knock it's simple - tap, tap, knock, tap, tap, knock. When I looked behind me, she had been pale as a ghost.

"Miss! Miss! We will be back." I shouted from my sea, standing up I headed for the door before Miss Gertrude yelled,

"Sit down!" I didn't listen to her; II just pointed toward Mila's paled-out face and grabbed her and headed for the door. The poor girl threw up two days' worth of foo; it seemed like. That's what happened when Josh, the kid in our class, showed up with a lunch that stunk up the classroom.

When I got to the bathroom, I could hear Mila already,

"Let me in!" I shouted from the other side of the stall door, she pulled it open slowly, and I went in with her, leaving the door open, but my body was blocking the view. I held her hair up for her and let her body release last night's toxins for as long as she needed; it was about 10 minutes. When she was done, she started to move her body to a standing position, so I backed up and gave her space. "So, you good or what?" I joked.

"I think so, yeah. I'm okay now." Mila confessed. We walked to the double sink, and she immediately started to rinse out her mouth and splashed her face with water. "Thank you"

"For what?" I replied

"For just always being there for me, all the time. Even when we were kids, you'd put yourself in front of me just to save my ass. So, thanks. I appreciate and love you, Ol."

"You're welcome." I jokingly salute her in a superhero stance. "And I love you too." We went in for a hug, and she rested there for a second before pulling away.

"I'm happy for you, but I can't wait until you come home." Mila boasted.

After brunch, Mila and Wyatt joined us for a walk on the harbour before they headed back home. Mila and I have never been the sentimental ones. We always knew we'd be seeing each other again, that we'd be face timing each other within hours of being home anyway. So it wasn't hard. We gave hugs and parted ways.

"I'll call you later, MUAH" She blew a kiss in our direction and waved as she and Wyatt drove off. It left us alone again, and part of me at that moment felt anxious about what was to come. For the good-byes, we'd have to endure.

Carter and I didn't like to talk about what would happen when the summer came to an end, and I thought that it was too painful to talk about. "We'll still see each other, right?" I'd say, and he would say, "Yes, of course. We're going to make it work." I had no doubts in my mind, but my stomach told another story.

♦ ♦ ♦

Chapter 12: The Last Day

The rest of the summer went by in a flash. We spent the time we could get together in each other's arms. The days slipped away from us, and as our departure became closer, the relationship we had built grew stronger.

The last time we spoke of that conversation was that night at the bonfire. The one about our unruly parting, the one happening because of Carter's choices, the things he had lied about all summer. Even though I knew it had burdened me when he lied, I also learned that time was creeping up on us and that our precious time was running out, which was terrifying. A conversation had to happen, and soon.

I couldn't sleep because I knew that the following day would be our last; with only a few hours of sleep, I awoke to birds chirping and Carter standing over the bed saying,

"Wake up, beautiful." I glanced at the clock shy of five o'clock in the morning.

"What could we possibly be doing this early? It's torture, you know. I thought you liked me. People who like me let me sleep." I pulled the blankets over my head and buried myself into the pillows.

"Get up!" He pulled the blankets off me and flopped onto the bed beside me. "I want to spend as much time as possible with you today. Please. Let's go. I don't want to miss it!" I sighed and got out of bed, it only took me about fifteen minutes to gather myself and get ready for the day, and we had taken our coffees to go. It was dark out, and the sun was ready to rise shortly. I could feel the crisp breeze; it smelt like sunrise. I can't explain that, but it did.

He brought me to the docks, and we got onto his boat. We drove about twenty minutes out, and I didn't say a word because it seemed like he was nervous. I knew he wasn't used to romantic gestures, and I could feel one coming. When we stopped, I heard a clan of birds in the distance; it sounded like swans. Sweet morning sounds of birdsongs. He told me to sit with him near the edge of the boat, and within ten minutes, the sky started to lighten up, and swans surrounded the boat.

"You pulled a Notebook?" I grinned so big and jumped into his arms, I hugged him so tightly, and even though I couldn't see his face then, I knew he was smiling just as big as I was.

Being with him felt like being 'home.' If someone were to ask me now, how would you describe the word, 'Home.' I would say, "Home is wherever he is." A single tear slipped down my cheek, and I quickly brushed it away, not wanting him to see it and have it somehow ruin our last day together.

"I would do anything for you; you know that, right, Olive?" He pulled a container filled with food to feed the swans, and we tossed it to them. I didn't need to speak any words. I just looked at him and shook my head. It was understood.

We spent the entire day in lovers' bliss. Not knowing what was to come, the pain we'd feel. After hours of laying in the sun, dancing in each other's arms, we could get out and do things.

We started at a remote waterfall. Carter drove us up to a docked area, nobody else was around, and it seemed private. He told me it was a surprise and even refused to tell me when I insisted because *'what if we get murdered out here, and I don't even know what's going on.'* He always found my paranoia of being murdered in every situation hilarious. As we stepped out of the boat and onto the dock, we were surrounded by forest. He told me I had to put on this blindfold and trust him, and I refused.

So before I could react, he picked me up, threw me over his shoulder, and ran toward the forested area. We couldn't breathe because we had been laughing so hard, so after a few minutes, he lowered me to the ground, pulled the blindfold out of his back pocket, and handed it to me, smirking. I didn't argue this time because curiosity had given in.

I closed my eyes and stepped forward. I had only been wearing my skin-tight yellow crop tank, so I could feel it when the wind picked up. When Carter grabbed my arms from behind me to help guide me the way— I got immediate goosebumps. The idea of not knowing should terrify me, but with him, I felt safe.

Before I knew it, we were approaching a waterfall, and I knew this because they were my favourites. I sensed it in the air, it became moist, and the splashing from the waterfall had been so loud it almost echoed. How did I not know this was here? The whole summer, I was staying in Elora, and I was only then seeing that hidden gem. It's a sound I could never forget. I stopped dead in my tracks and ripped the blindfold off. "Not yet!" Carter panicked, but he could tell I was so excited that panic washed away in seconds. He didn't care.
I ran toward the edge, grabbing Carter's hand to come with me and then looked up to see the most brilliant waterfall, with such a satin blue that it made your eyes not want to look away. It drizzled onto the rocks at the bottom that had formed into a pool.

Things felt so good between us at that moment, the way we ran down the steep hill to get to the bottom; we stripped each other's clothes off and dove right into the water. We had no worries. We stayed entangled in each other for what felt like a lifetime. We floated in the water and indulged in each other, telling each other funny stories from our childhood, and when things got too deep, he would flick water at me or try to push me over, making me laugh.

I brought my polaroid camera, and I even made him smile for a couple of photos. A massive part of me wanted to cry right then and there and beg him not to leave me, but I held it back and tried my hardest to enjoy what time we had because I knew I'd be crying for hours, days, and even months after he left for the Army.

Before I had time to process it, we were standing outside the train station. Not yet ready to walk through and say goodbye, possibly forever. I stood there silently for a few minutes before I cried. I could taste the tears almost instantly, reminding me how hard I had been crying over this man.

I felt like a part of me was being ripped away. I sobbed into Carter's chest for minutes before I could calm myself. Everything started to become so *real.* I wasn't ready for Carter to leave, yet I was - going back to Toronto while he went off to whatever 'training classes' his dad signed him up for to prepare himself for the Army.

"I'm going to really fucking miss you." He shouted. I pulled him as close to me as I could and held on tight.

"Ditto, baby." I wiped the tears from my eyes and pushed my hair out of my face. I started to pull away from him, but I couldn't budge. He didn't let me.

"I just need a few more minutes like this." He rested his head on top of mine. "I know it's a long time, but I need you to wait for me, baby." Carter pulled out from our hug and held onto the side of my arms, he looked deeply into my eyes, and I could see them fill with water; he was going to cry. "I love you so fucking much, Olive. Please wait for me."

"I'll wait forever If I have to." I pulled into him tightly and slipped a polaroid photo into his pocket without him knowing, with a note on it. I wanted him to keep a piece of us with him when he went off to become a hero.

"I'll see you in a year, baby."

♦ ♦ ♦

Chapter 13: The Reunion

"So you were supposed to meet him yesterday and didn't show up? Why was that?" Agnus asks.

"I just got too scared, maybe he had moved on, and I would embarrass myself. I have never even tried to write or reach out. It's been an entire year since I've seen him. What if he didn't show up? I was scared, so I did what I do best - fuck up." I say, sounding defeated.

"Well, while we're here, why don't you explain why you backed out?" She insists.

1 DAY EARLIER

I woke to the sound of my alarm blaring in my ears. It was 6:59 am. My regular time is to wake up before I start my day and get ready for work. But it would be unique, and I had it all planned out.

I couldn't wait to see Carter again. I pushed all my fears away and woke with a smile. I jumped to my feet and walked to my kitchen, where I flicked the button to start my coffee pot. I headed to the shower, turned the water on, brushed my teeth, and stripped down. I got into the shower, and everything I had done since I opened my eyes was smooth, calm, and collected. I couldn't help but get that strange feeling, the one I get before a bad day is going to happen. "Not fucking today. No way". I kept telling myself.

I showered and got the outfit I had placed out so nicely and slipped into it. I grabbed my phone and went back to the kitchen. I needed coffee. I made my regular, two sugars, two milk. The feeling started eating away at me. I told my brain,

'*You cannot win today. You will not win today.*'

I had a shorter shift yesterday than usual, so I went to work and dodged people all day. I avoided anything that could turn the day upside down. I wanted to see Carter, which I've wanted since we separated 12 months three ago.
Was that some lousy omen?

'Please give me a fucking sign. And I will go home and hide all day.'

My inner voice repeated this to me all day.
I had been counting down the days until I could see him since we last parted, and I felt like my body was telling me something awful would happen. It took me minutes to realize that I had been picking at the skin around the edges of my nails, causing me to bleed. Shit. Maybe it was a sign I shouldn't go.

I couldn't take it. I left work and headed home. Walking down the street, I put my AirPods in; I turned my favourite podcast on, *Dark History.* I tried to talk these thoughts out of my head, but my stomach ached, sending shivers through my entire body. My head was pounding like nobody's business, and I felt awful. Beyond the sound of Bailey Sarian, I hear screams. I pulled my air-pods out, and that's when I saw it.

I stopped dead in my tracks, and I saw it when I looked over for more than a second. Someone had jumped from the fifteenth floor and landed less than 10 feet from me.

It was a fucking sign. Shivers went down my spine, and vomit flew out of my mouth. I couldn't stop it. This was a sign if I ever needed one. I wasn't going. I was going home and hiding under my covers. This brings me to fall asleep at 7 pm, a bucket of chicken and Cheetos in hand. When I awoke at midnight, depressed and alone, it kicked in. That's when I pulled a bottle out of the cabinet and ended up at the train station, asleep and hungover early in the morning.

Present

"Life is a series of lessons and choices; what you chose yesterday doesn't determine what you chose today. So, maybe yesterday wasn't a great day, maybe the world was telling you not to go, but today is a new day. You can change your choice and make a new one moving forward. It sounds like that boy was head over heels for you, and if that's the case, Sweetie, nothing has changed. How will you ever know if you don't give it a shot?" Agnus sounds the most serious now than she has our entire conversation.

I always knew my decision, but things became clear to me right then and there. I was in love with Carter; nothing else mattered. The risks were worth it because, in the end, the reward could be much more significant.

"Oh my god, I have to go. I have to go now. What the fuck am I doing?" I jump off my couch and run toward my bedroom. I grab my suitcase and start throwing things in there without even thinking.

'What if he doesn't take me back?' I was supposed to meet him yesterday, but he didn't come.

"He's going to take you back. Stop it."

'What if he moved on?'

'He didn't move on; get over yourself.'

My mind is racing, my thoughts fighting with one another. I don't let it stop me, though. I manage to pack the essentials and head for the door.

"Thank you, Agnus." I smile wholeheartedly. "I have a train to catch." I pick up my cell phone, toss it into my purse, grab my suitcase and open my front door, motioning Agnus to walk ahead.

I push through the crowded streets of Toronto, my heart still racing, and my stomach flips. I keep a slow but steady pace, so Agnus can stick with me since she, too, needs to catch a train. I have 6 minutes to make it to the next train, or I'm stuck here waiting for the next one, and my heart and head cannot take it. I need to go before my head catches up with my heart, and I go back to my apartment.

It takes us four minutes to get to the top of the stairs to the subway leading down to the train I need to catch. People are pushing all over, trying to reach their destination. Nobody realizes what I'm up against, though. My heart is on the line. Agnus shouts, "Go, Sweetie! It was so very nice to have met you." There are so many voices and bodies all around us. I can just make out what she says. I give her a big hug and squeeze.

"Thank you." I pull back, smile, and dart down the stairs, pushing bodies out of my way and keeping my grip tight on my suitcase.

I reach the bottom of the steps and run through people but slowly inch back and forth through the crowd as I go. I see the train I need only ten feet

away, so I move in that direction. The doors open, and the trains fill within seconds, people pushing their way into the doors. I don't make it quite in time, and as I run to the door entry, they shut.
I'm crushed, defeated. Whatever you call it, I feel it. I let go of my bag, pull my hands to my face, and start crying.

"Olive?"

I look up, and when I do, I see him. Carter. He's standing across the train station, smiling at me. I can tell it's him, he's grown his hair, with a bit of a beard. It looks good on him.

I can't move. I stand there, tears streaming down my face. He's smiling, and then mouths,

"Hi, baby."

I don't care anymore, I leave my suitcase where it is, and I run into his arms and promise I'm not letting him go this time.

Lucky for me, as we reunited, the local guitarist that plays in the Subway had been there; I have gotten to know him over the years. His name is Roger, and he is very talented. As I ran into Carter's arms, Roger pulled out his guitar and strummed the chorus to All my Loving by the Beatles, singing along with it.

All my loving I will send to you
All my loving,

Darling, I'll be true.

It only took moments for Carter and me to get swept up at the moment, and ironically it only took us what felt like seconds to make it back to my apartment. We stood outside the door, and I had to break my lips from his to get my keys out and open this annoying door. I'm shaking, rattling the key - it couldn't be any less sexy. Carter takes the keys from my hands, "May I?" Holy shit, the subway has terrible lighting because I see him standing here - right now, in front of this man, in my grunge-ass apartment hallway. He's slightly aged, he's grown out a bit of facial hair, and the hair on his head is a few inches longer. I feel the heat between my legs and a bit of cramp. God, he's sexy.

"Don't do that." He says,

"What?"

"Bite your lip like that; let me open this door first." He struggles to open, just as I do.

"What the fuck is wrong with thls thing?" I feel my cheeks red, and the door swings open. Carter grabs my hand, pulls me into the door, and shuts it behind him. He turns around, drops his bag onto the floor, and slips off his shoes and jacket; before he can turn around, I'm behind him, up on my tiptoes, and I whisper in his ear,

"I missed you." He turns toward me and licks his lips.

"I've more than missed you, baby. I'm aching for you." He leans down and puts his hand on my lower back, pulling me into him. It only took a second for me to feel the bulge in his pants, and I wrap my arms around his neck and kiss him, only this time it was not the sensual one we had at the subway; this one is filled with want and need. He grabs my legs and pulls me up, so I wrap my legs around his waist. We don't stop for air, only to remove pieces of clothing. He takes a few steps, and now my back is leaning against a wall, his lips still mashed against mine. I can feel the bristle of his beard scraping against my cheeks and down my neck. I moan as he hits the right spot on my neck.

He kissed me exactly how I wanted and needed to be kissed. I craved to make it last longer, and we didn't stop until we made it to the bedroom and fell asleep in each other's arms.

I wake in the middle of the night, lying on Carter's bare chest. His mouth is slightly curved open, and he's breathing loudly but fast asleep. I slide out from under his left arm and carefully place it down, not wanting to wake him. I creep to the kitchen to get a drink because, after all of those sexual activities, I'm parched. I tiptoe out of the kitchen because the floors are old and creek loud when the house is in quiet mode. “Baby,” Carter stands there, groggy from sleep, running his hands over his chiselled beard. “You alright?” He puts his hands on my bare hips, only covered by a peach-coloured thong and his t-shirt. I get up on my tippy-toes and wrap my arms around his neck,

“I'm good, just thirsty.” I pull myself up and wrap my legs around him. I drag my tongue down his neck and suck slowly on his soft skin. He moans ever so slightly, and his body tenses around me. I hop down, “I need a shower; I’m filthy.” I take a few steps forward and look back at him, “Coming with?”

I ask, shrugging my shoulders as I pull his t-shirt off my body and slide the thong down, kicking it off to the side. Carter runs up behind me, grabbing me playfully, “I’m coming with you, even though it's 3 am and we need sleep.” He tugs on my ear with his teeth.

I take my time with this one and make him want me; I make him ache for me. We enter my tiny bathroom, the toilet to the right, and the shower/bath is straight ahead, with a little sink to the left. I bend over slightly, turn the water on, and carefully adjust it to the right temperature. As he approaches behind me, Carter slowly drags his finger up my thigh, and I slap his hand away.

“Wait!” I wink, his jaw drops, and he mocks me,

“Tease. Fine.”

I turn to the sink and look at myself in the mirror. I slowly pull my hairbrush out, lifting my arms so he can see my breasts. When I look into the mirror, Carter is standing behind looking at me, biting his lip. He slides his boxers down and takes no time before he is pushed up behind me. He puts his right hand on my hip and drags his left up my torso, stopping at my breast before lightly pinching my nipple. I released a soft moan and pushed backward, leaning into him, *"Carter."* He rests his hand on my throat, just under my chin and then tilts my head slightly, facing him before he leans in and sticks his tongue into my mouth, savoring every moment. We barely made it to the shower before rounds two and three started.

♦ ♦ ♦

Chapter 14: The Wedding

Well, today is the big day. I awake to birds chirping and the sun glaring down on my bare skin, sending warmth through my body instead of the chills I feel as I wake up in my dingy Toronto apartment. Hotels have always been the ultimate comfort. The beds are comfortable, the sheets are always fresh and clean, and the view from this one is spectacular. Before rolling out of bed, I glance to the bedside, looking for my cell phone, but instead-I see a coffee cup with a note leaning on it.

"For you, my love. See you later XO - C."

Weddings are many things. They are joy, stress, laughter, and tears and are one of the most marvellous things to happen. Two people, bound together, showing their love for one another.

Growing up around the streets of Toronto, I saw many weddings in the parks, hotels and churches. I had this erratic love for brides and finding the perfect person to fall in love with. All I wanted was to be them or a part of their day. I would cut out brides' photos from magazines, glue them all to a board, and pair them with an image of a field of tulips. My favourite flower. I would say, 'I want to get married there!'

I called it my "One Day" board. Maybe my friends and family thought it was silly, but it made me pretty remarkable. I didn't want to be a doctor or a police officer, and I didn't want to be a scientist. I just wanted to be a bride and someone to love me unconditionally. Part of that was from all my daddy issues. I always wondered what the truth was between my Mom and biological father, but I just wanted to know if there was any love there, if I was a product of love and affection and not a drunken error between them. All I know is that my Mom says it's better if I don't know the details.

Despite my upbringing and love life, or lack of - until Carter. Here I am today, and although it's not my wedding, it's my best friend's. I'm a maid of honour, and that's the second-best job I could ask for today. I throw on my maid of honour house coat and fluffy slippers and head to Mila's room so we can get ready together.

As I burst into the doors of her room, I catch her and Wyatt intertwined in each other's lips, not even noticing my presence, so I cough very loudly. "Excuse me! This is bad luck." I rush toward him, flailing my hands at Wyatt as I shoo him away. "Out!"

"I couldn't help myself." Wyatt giggles and exits the room. And I stare at my best friend with those *'what the heck are you doing? You know I believe in superstitions eyes*

"Bad. Luck. Can you believe me for once?" I emphasize the words so she can hear me.

"Oh, relax, Ol. It's fine." Mila shrugs and walks to the mini-bar sitting under the window filled with mimosas, ready to start the day. "TO LOVE!" She picks up two glasses and passes one to me; right before we clink glasses, the rest of the bridal party arrives, and the day commences.

Carter

I am thinking of you today, my love. I'm not sure I'll be able to make it. Grams has just passed away, and Mom is a mess. I can't leave her. Let me know when you're getting ready to go. I love you.

I knew how close Carter was with his grams, so a text back wouldn't work for me. I need to hear his voice, so I sneak to my room and lock the door behind me.

"Hi... Carter. Are you alright? What happened?" I say frantically.

"I'll be right back, Mom. Drink some water.. please. Hi baby, hold on." I can hear him shuffling around and a sliding door open. So he must be going outside for this conversation. "Sorry, my love. They don't know what happened. She slipped outside during a walk and wound up in the hospital. She was fine, and then she wasn't. Mom's devastated. But don't let me ruin Mila and Wyatt's day. I'll pick you up later, okay?"

"Okay.. are you alright? You didn't answer my question." I can tell by his voice that he's feeling off.

"No, it feels a bit sudden. I had hoped you would have met her and we could have all made more memories together. I'm shaken up, but I'm trying to stay strong for Mom, and I miss you." The sound of his voice on the other end makes my heart break a little bit, and if this day weren't so important, I would have left in a heartbeat.

"I'm so sorry. I love you, and she loved you so much that I'm certain of. I'm sorry I didn't meet her, but I'm sure she was lovely. I can't say much to make you feel better right now, but I love you."

"I love you too." He says, but he sounds so defeated and tired. So I try to cheer him up in the best way I know how.

"And I'm not wearing any undies today, just for you…." I swear I can hear him smile.

"I love you, Olive. And now I really can't wait to see you later."

"Byyyyyeeeee." I plant 100 quick kisses into the phone before I hang up.

Well, the show must go on. So on I went. Today should be a spectacular day; my best friend is getting married. Also, the love of my life is suffering from a significant loss. As happy as I am for today, I can't wait to cuddle up to Carter later and watch movies together.

I smiled and laughed the day away and cried during the vows, which I cannot repeat because It makes me a blubbering mess. I surprisingly held it all together really well, that's until the end of the night came close, I was one too many cosmos deep, and it was my turn for the speech.

I promptly stand up, grab the mic, tap it, and then laugh awkwardly.

"Anyway, yikes. Hey everyone, most of you know who I am - but for those who don't, my name is Olive, and I'm Milas's best friend. We have been best friends for more than half our lives, which means we're sisters, right?" I look over to Mila, leaning into Wyatt's chest, and they both have a glass of champagne in hand. I was looking over at them with a nervous smile on my face.

"Mila and I have fantasized about this day since we were seven. Who'd we'd marry, where, and when? Of course, it was all outrageous ideas, but we planned it nonetheless. Mila told me never to speak of this, but come on; I've been saving this secret for this *exact* moment.

"So, it goes like this. Picture it, 12-year-old Mila. Dead set on marrying Justin Bieber. They were going to marry in the Bahamas and have 'lots and lots' babies."

Milas's eyes widen, and she mouths 'How dare you' Wyatt says, "I want to hear this," and grins down at Mila. She laughs, but her face starts to turn all shades of red.

"Her wedding with Justin Bieber was going to be fantastic, she'd be escorted in a carriage, and there would be doves and a huge wedding cake made to look just like them. They'd ride off together and spend weeks on an extravagant honeymoon, picked by her new Hubby." I wink over at her and

laugh." *Okay, okay. It didn't happen, but she found something much better with Wyatt. Since the day they met, something had changed in her. A newfound happiness that was because he had entered her life. Your love story is one for the books. Congratulations. To my best friend and her soulmate, Wyatt. I love you. And I can't wait until you have many babies."* I raise my glass, and everyone joins in.

Finally, the night is coming to an end. I'm sitting at the head table, exhausted after such an extravagant day. "Go home. Get some rest," Mila approaches beside me. And then wraps her arms around my chest from behind and pecks me a kiss on the top of my head. "You are exhausted. You have done more than enough today. Thank you, Ol. I love you." I stand up and face her and give them the biggest smile.

"You're married!" I screech, and then she cries back, and we jump up and down together like two excited toddlers on Christmas morning.

"I think I owe you congratulations, Mrs. Camson.." I know that voice. I know it very well. I look behind my shoulder and see Carter behind me. He steps past me first and hugs Mila, and then grabs me. We do this weird threesome hug, and then we hear Wyatt in the background,

"Wow. You guys are hugging without me????" He laughs and runs up and joins in on it.

THE NEXT DAY

Things are quiet between us, and that's okay. I know that Carter doesn't like feeling defeated and helpless, and this situation was out of his hands ultimately. Grams was fine until she wasn't. All I know is that she lived in the city and that I would see her once a week. Her husband had passed on, so she was alone but completely capable of her day-to-day tasks on her own, and as far as I've heard - she was very stubborn, which is why she always preferred to live alone. *'Carry on,'* she'd always say with a big grin.

The day's task is going over to Gram's apartment to retrieve photos to display at her funeral. "You don't have to come with me, you can relax today if you want to." Carter sat on the bed next to me; he had come out of the shower with only a towel wrapped around his waist, drops of water sliding down his skin; it was getting harder to focus on anything else, to be honest. "You with me?" Carter smiles and turns to me, cupping my face with his big hands and giving me the most passionate kiss.

"I'm coming with you. You can't convince me otherwise. Let me help you, okay?" I insist.

After a dreaded subway ride, we arrived back in the city from Elora. No matter how often I've ridden on it or will again, I'll never get used to it. It stinks, and people are so pushy. I want to shout, 'back the fuck up,' but you can't do that these days without getting stabbed or spat on. So, I keep to myself and judge them all in my head. 'Ha! Take that'

It takes us about ten minutes from where we got off on foot to arrive at her apartment. Once we get inside his grams' apartment, the vibe changes. Carter starts to pace around her apartment, not knowing where to start, and I'm hyper-focused on making sure Carter is okay today. "This won't take long. I know where she keeps her albums." We walked into the living room, an open concept with lots of browns and reds. My eyes focus directly on a painting behind the couch; I take a few steps toward it and turn on the end table light. The image is something I've never seen before, and the picture isn't entirely clear; it's a mix of reds and browns, much like the furniture in this place - which, come to think of it, probably was all made around this masterpiece. If you squint your eyes and tilt your head slightly to the right, you could make out two hands trying to grasp each other, mixed in with thick paint strokes. It was so beautiful and barely noticeable unless you took the time to look at it.

"Got' em'." He sits on the couch beside me and opens the book. "Grams painted that." He looks up at the painting that I can't get my eyes off. Wow. This grams sure was an extraordinary lady.

"It's beautiful. I've never seen anything like it before." I sit next to him and glance over. These photos are old, and you can tell she was very young. "Look at that! Where is she here?"

"I think that's Florida with my Gramps, shortly after my mom was born." He grabs a few photos out and keeps flipping the pages. Going over all the old memories he could remember. We gather a huge pile of pictures near the end of Book Four. Only this time, when he flips the page, I'm stunned. I'm staring at a picture, and it looks like someone had taken it a few years before I met Carter, as he looked slightly younger than he did when we met. I slap my hand on the photo and make a weird dinosaur-type sound.

"Holy shit!"

"What, Olive? What's wrong? Did you see a bug or something? I know how much you hate spiders." He jokes,

"No.. not a spider. Who is that?" My palms are getting sweaty, and I'm feeling nauseous now.

"Who... Grams?"

"Hold on. Grams? What's her name?" At the same time, we both speak

"Agnus"

♦ ♦ ♦

Epilogue

Beep. Beep. Beep. Beep. Beep. Beep.
Drip. Drip. Drip.

"You're doing great, Olive. One more push!" Nurse Corena says in a calming voice. I hardly notice any features about her because I'm consumed with the burning pain as I'm crowning. The hospital room is dull, and the only sounds and colour is from the copious amounts of nurses, doctors and all their instruments. I don't care where anyone is or what anyone sees. Even though I'm laying spread eagle with my feet in stirrups like a damn horse, I don't care. My vagina is on complete display. In any other circumstance aside from birth, this would be a mortifying experience.

"There's the head! Breathe, and then one big more big push" the nurse starts to sound excited. Carter grips my hand harder. He's been squeezing it the whole time and wiping the sweat off my forehead with a damp cloth.

"Our baby is almost here, Olive, you're amazing, I love you, breathe, baby" I'm so amazed at how he's been throughout my entire birth, he never shied away, and he wanted to be present for all of it. I don't know if I could have done it without him. As prepare for my final push, I'm overcome with a burning ring feeling in my downstairs and immense pain in my lower back and abdomen.

I count myself down in my head. 3. 2. 1. I push with all my might and let out a huge scream, probably mixed with swear words. I look up at Carter, and the look on his face assures me our baby has been brought earthside. Immediately they place this tiny little human on my chest.

"Your beautiful baby girl is excited to meet you," the doctor says, and I start to weep.

"A daughter," I say, sniffling and looking up at Carter, who also has tears swelling in his eyes. She is perfect, with her tiny button nose and pale skin, but her eyes are all her Daddy. My body is exhausted, but I don't want this moment to end.

"Do you want to cut the cord?" one of the nurses said, looking at Carte. She didn't need an answer from him as hestood over our baby in a blink of an eye. Within seconds, they swept her off my chest and took her to her little cot, where the doctors ran some tests. I watched her the whole time.

"She's perfect, Olive, just like you," Carter says, kissing me on the forehead. I hardly notice the nurse who is still examining my private area. She explained to me I'd have to deliver the placenta and

I would most likely need a few stitches due to tearing, and honestly, that was the worst part. I could feel every tug, making me sick to my stomach. When they were finished fixing me up and assured me our baby was perfectly healthy, I was told I could try to breastfeed. Which is a weird experience, to have a nurse grab your boob and shove your nipple into your child's mouth. "Like this" they would repeat, over and over again. I know with some practice, I'd be able to handle it on my own.

After Carter and I spent some time with her, he looked at me with our daughter in his arms "rest, baby," he said. As much as I wanted to stay awake and soak everything in, my body was fighting against me. Within seconds of closing my eyes, I drifted off to sleep with the image of the love of my life holding our perfect baby.

When I open my eyes and look up to old ceiling boards, stained yellow in spots from leaks, and when I turn my head, I see the machines I'm hooked up to, an IV dripping next to me that's connected to my left hand. It takes me a few seconds to remember where I am; I'm at the hospital.

I look to my left and see Carter, fast asleep, sitting in the chair. It all comes to me when I notice the bassinet with a baby girl wearing a pink bowed hat on her tiny little head.

I sit there for a few minutes to admire the man lying before me and the baby girl who just entered this world- our baby girl. I can't believe this day has finally come; I'm so overfilled with joy, I try to pull myself to sit up so I can get a better look at her, but the aches flow through the lower half of my body when I remember the tearing of my lower region.

I start clicking buttons until the bed starts to sit me up. I stop to take breaths because my pain is brutal, so with each inch, it moves; I take a deep breath. I look over at the clock, and it's 5:56 am. The next nurse will be here in five minutes with my pain medication. I groan in pain, and Carter rushes to the side of the bed when he opens his eyes and sees me struggling to get up.

"Baby, slow down. Why didn't you ask me for help?" He grabs me slowly and helps me adjust to the bed so I can sit straight.

"I wanted to see her, and I can't move." I sigh in defeat and pout. He looks down at her, smiles, and then looks back at me.

"She sure is perfect, isn't she, mama?" He rubs my back with one hand, reaches down, and grazes her cheek with his other. She squirms awake, and he grabs her gently and kisses her tiny little nose before handing her to me.

"Hi, little one." I smile, cuff her tiny head in my hand, and hold her back with my other arm. Carter leans into our small beautiful baby girl and me.

"I love you, Ol. You did an amazing job."

"I can't believe she's here." I snuggle into him, and we all fit perfectly together. "I know what I want to name her." He moves slightly so he's facing me.

"Yeah?"

"Elyse, Your Grammy's middle name." I look up at him, and a tear runs down his cheek.

“Elyse.”

“Elyse.” I smile.

♦ ♦ ♦

Bonus Chapter

Carter

Past,

She doesn't know how much it hurts to walk away from her. I almost didn't go. But my life has always been a series of plans, and I've always followed through. As much as I hate it, I get it from my dad. I know it's dangerous and life-threatening, but I've wanted to do it since I was a little kid and plan on making my way through the next three years with flying colours.

Olive doesn't know that the second I had laid eyes on her was earlier than the moment I saved her, which I still kick my ass for; I wish that I could have been there, even a fucking few minutes earlier, to save her from that trauma.

The first time I saw Olive, she had stepped out of the motel and looked at her phone before walking down the street. I was going for a run when I noticed her, and I hid out of sight; I wasn't ready for her to see me until I could figure out who this shining star was that had come into town. It took me until I saw her heading toward Elora Reef when I realized she was the intern Ronnie had spoken of, who was here for the summer.

She was seriously the most beautiful girl I had ever seen. I know it's cliche as fuck, but it is true. My dick ached almost instantly when I saw her flip her hair to her back and bend down to tie her shoelaces. I couldn't work up the nerves to approach her, and I felt weird after, like I had almost creepily stalked her to her workplace.

I knew I had to wait before figuring out what she was about. When I saw her leave Elora Reef, I hurried inside and asked Ronnie anything I could, but he just nagged me, but he told me Nancy had spoken to her, so I knew my next step was to find my sister, Lynn, who was Nancy's friend, and ask her what it was about.

The second Olive agreed to be mine, my world became our world, my heart became our heart, and my life became our life. She means more than everything to me, and I cannot wait to spend the rest of my life with her — one day.

I step onto the train and then find my seat, so I sit down; I see Olive smiling and waving out the window. I can tell she's crying, but I smile and wave back. I hold my hand by my heart to let her know she's always with me, and then I turn around. It hurts too much to sit there and stare at her and pretend I don't know she's breaking apart just 20 feet away.

I put my hand in my pocket to grab my phone and message her again, telling her how much I love her. I pull my phone out with a polaroid photo, and it falls to the floor. It's a smiling photo of her and me together at the waterfall. The back says,

What're three years? Until then, I love you, XO.

Without even trying, a tear slides down my cheek.

I don't know what I ever did to deserve a girl like Olive, but I can damn well guarantee she will be on my mind until we meet again. I hope and pray that she feels the same when the time comes.

NOW

I've been waiting for this moment since she walked away from me three years ago. Here we are, and I can't seem to move my legs. It's 1:56 pm, and we're set to meet at 2 pm. She and I agreed that we wouldn't keep in contact to make things easier while apart. We figured it was a clean break; if she decided to move on, it wouldn't be any pressure. I reached out to Jay only months ago, who ensured she got the note I had sent her. To remind her to meet me today. At our spot.

As the minutes go by, I get worried more and more that she won't show up today, that she'll have changed her mind. Or that Jay didn't get my note to give her the other message; maybe she still needs to get it. All I know is I can't let go of her now.
I waited for hours, way more than past the time I had hoped to meet. I realized that Ellie was not coming. I head back home, and on the way, I see all the excited neighbours who had hoped I would go home after three long years in combat to be with the love of my life.
Typically, I would be going back, but I hurt my leg a year ago and have been doing nothing until my contract was over and they sent me home. Sent me home like it was just a summer camp I had visited, and I was finished with them. But the truth is, it changed me. It changed who I am; the only thing It didn't change was my love for that witty, sassy girl - My Olive.

I get the odd smile or nod as I head for my parent's home and walk up the stairs. I could tell the disappointment from everyone as I returned without her.

Sour as ever, I walk through the front doors. I try to brainstorm a million reasons why Olive wouldn't have shown up today, and my mind is telling me she's fallen out of love with me and moved on. On the other hand, my heart is telling me something entirely different.

I know what I have to do. So I grab a bag from my closet and pack the bag as fast as I can. As I go to swing my bedroom door open, I run into my father, who stands still as a brick in front of my door. "Oh, son. I've just come to speak to you. I'm sorry this girl didn't show up, but there's no reason to pout…."

I push past him. "Fuck off!" I shout as I run down the stairs and head for my car.

I'm going to get my girl.

♦ ♦ ♦

Thank you so much for reading Carter and Olive's story, I hope that you enjoyed reading it as much as I loved writing it.

Manufactured by Amazon.ca
Bolton, ON

32691274R00120